If Only For One Night

By Erik McGowan

If Only for One Night

Copyright © 2024 by Erik McGowan

All rights reserved.

No part of this publication may be reproduced, distributed, or transmitted in any form or by any means, including photocopying, recording, or other electronic or mechanical methods, without the prior written permission of the publisher, except as permitted by U.S. copyright law. For permission requests, contact Erik McGowan at mcgowsquared@gmail.com.

The story, all names, characters, and incidents portrayed in this production are fictitious. No identification with actual persons (living or deceased), places, buildings, and products is intended or should be inferred.

Book Cover by Erik McGowan

Edited by Erik McGowan

First edition 2024

ISBN

Paperback: 978–1–7326545–2–5

Ebook: 978–1–7326545–3–2

Acknowledgments

Very big thanks to Vicki McGowan-Smith, Derek McGowan Sr, Derek McGowan II, Nikkia Tia Carter, LaTonya Simon, Whitney Cunningham, Jowanna Malone, Emani Carter, Chris Franklin, Ta'mi Clark, Mitch Vitullo, Divya, Andrea Boston, Kenneth Goodman, Sheena Crawley, and Dario, for either helping with the beta process, listening to my ideas, reading and reviewing my previous works, checking to see if my translations were correct, or encouraging me to finish this project. I appreciate you all.

Table of Contents

Prologue - The Contract

Chapter 1 - Old Friends

Chapter 2 - Lust

Chapter 3 - Dusk

Chapter 4 - The Urumi

Chapter 5 - Lord of Violence

Chapter 6 - Hounds of Hell

Chapter 7 - Pride

Chapter 8 - Black as Pitch

Chapter 9 - Bricks and Mortar

Chapter 10 - Rabenmutter

Chapter 11 - Sloth

Chapter 12 - Envy

Chapter 13 - No Light

Chapter 14 - If Only For One Night

Chapter 15 - Wrath

Chapter 16 - Coming Dawn

Chapter 17 - Fraud

Chapter 18 - Dumbwaiter

Chapter 19 - Epilogue

-Prologue-
THE CONTRACT

The Sun burned the sky and scorched the desert below, but Ava paid the heat no mind. Its intense rays affected her like a breeze in the vacuum space. Her mind was focused, searching her surroundings for other occupants that usually littered the area. Weary wanderers by the dozens shuffled through the ever-shifting dunes.

The first few days ended with no success. Ava saw plenty of scattered nomads marching through the desert with the swollen sun beating down on their backs or faces. They staggered and shuffled their feet as they passed. Some had humped backs and crooked necks from their constant downward stares. Their bodies were draped in tattered clothing that stuck to their sweaty sun-scorched skin like shredded paper on wet glass. Each of them was on their own journey, searching for salvation from the tremendous heat, but there would be no such thing in such a place as this.

In a sense, they were the lucky ones. Their never-ending march kept them from meeting the same fate as those who were foolish enough to stop for a break. For each one that continued to march, they were saved from the torment that befell any sad soul that could not continue any longer or who outright refused to travel another single step.

A lengthy thrashing, amongst other unspeakable tortures, fell upon those proud few who decided that they had traveled far enough. Until, like the rest, they realized that the punishment of constant walking or crawling was a much better choice. They would drag themselves on their stomachs across the hot, coarse sand to start the slow process of moving again. But eventually, they would force themselves back to their feet to labor on. Ava has watched it happen several times already. The person would stop for a quick break, a pause to get their bearings, or to partner up with one or two others hoping that their collective shadows would give the other some semblance of relief, which never worked. Then, like clockwork, the Others would come, which would be followed by their traumatizing screams and the spilling of blood.

Those mouth-breathing saps would do or try anything to escape the heat. Some took to digging like an excited dog burying a bone.

Their mouths were agape with dry blistered tongues flopped over cracked lips. Their worn hands shoveled through the baking sands, hoping to find lower temperatures hidden beneath. One or two had climbed into their newly created hip hole only to find that the pit only grew hotter the further down they dug. The truly foolish dug ditches like a prospector. Digging holes every several feet on their pseudo-hunch the next chosen spot will be the one they have been looking for. Maybe they would find some trace of water that might quench their thirst. Those few were insane, and that kind of insanity would never do for what Ava was planning. So, Ava kept walking, bypassing those stubborn lunatics until she found the last piece of her puzzle.

The next day was more of the same. Delirious from dehydration and their dismal situation, the tortured continued their march to nowhere. The skin on their upper backs, chest, forehead, or any other exposed body part peeled like lead paint. Flakes of skin would often quiver from gusts of wind like autumn leaves and fall to the ground in the same fashion. With the gusts of humid wind came a barrage of particles that assaulted their damaged skin and became trapped in the corners of their eyes.

Ava saw a figure in the distance, quivering through the heatwaves. He or she, Ava could not tell just yet, walked at what seemed like a casual pace. It was almost a strut. Head high, chest up, they used a hand to shield their eyes from the light of the blazing Sun. She was intrigued. Ava changed direction and walked towards the figure. She watched them closely as she closed the distance. They looked around seemingly for a landmark of some kind. It was a man, middle-aged, still dressed in his business suit. With all the tremendous heat, he had unbuttoned his jacket, but his tie was still tied tight around his neck.

Ava's speedy approach down the nearby dune from less than a mile away caught his eye. He waved both hands above his head, wildly, like a person close to drowning. His face brightened. He looked more hopeful than the ones she had seen earlier. He jogged over to her, kicking up pounds of sand as he went.

"Hello," he shouted, cupping his hands around his mouth as he ran.

Ava continued to walk at an average pace. Her face pointed in a slightly different direction as if she did not notice, but her eyes watched the man like a hawk.

He grew closer. He was close enough to not need his hands to amplify his voice but at a distance where shouting still felt like a necessity. "You there. Have you come from nearby?" He slowed down on his approach. Breathing heavily, he stopped a couple of feet from Ava. "Is there a village or city back there?" He pointed towards the assumed area she came from.

Ava did not speak. She stared at him. His wingtips were partially hidden in the shifting sands. His face dripped with sweat.

"I'm sorry, my name is Andre Taylor." He reached into the inside of his jacket for his business card case. Andre gave a quick smile, "I'm so sorry. What am I thinking? I've seemed to be walking around in circles for hours now. The sun's been sitting on high all day. I can't tell east from west. You're the first person I've seen so far." He wiped his forehead with the sleeve of his jacket. The fabric darkened from the sweat.

Ava wondered what he had done to get himself stuck on this level.

"I need to get back to...," he pointed back with his thumb. "Where are we? My memory is a little hazy. I've taken several trips to the desert before. This past year I stayed in Dubai for three weeks setting up a major deal. Lots of zeros behind it." Andre nodded with a smile. "They took me everywhere. We rode some four-wheelers… but I, I was always with a tour guide." He smiled. "So, when I noticed my outfit, well… I must have gotten lost or separated from the group. Sometimes I drink. A couple of gin and tonics to get the blood flowing and the party going." Andre laughed. Ava did not. "I figure, I must have drunk a little too much this time around and walked in the wrong direction." He mimicked shaking a shot glass in front of his mouth as he looked from side to side. "I—" He finally stopped talking and started observing.

The newcomer, the woman who now stood a good foot or two in front of him, was not sweating at all. Her brown skin did not have the lightest sheen of moisture, what his mother would call, a woman's glow. In fact, from what he could tell, the woman did not look hot at all. The woman looked more like she had been taking a stroll through the park on a barely warm spring day, not somebody who was standing in the middle of a desert. What was even more odd to him was the fact that all of her clothes were completely clean with not a hint of dust. Even her multicolored high-top sneakers looked brand new. His brow tightened. He opened his mouth.

"Before you ask, don't," Ava said, "It's not important. What I've got to say is. We've got a good...," she glanced over his shoulder. "Twenty minutes to talk before some of the Others show up to motivate you into moving. Right now—"

While she talked, Andre looked over both of his shoulders, seeing nothing but endless sand and the clear blue sky. "Others?" He said with a hint of excitement. "Will they arrive in vehicles or on some camels? I've never ridden on one of those before. I've heard they smell worse than the elephant pen at the zoo." He curled his lip to the thought. "Not that I'm picky." He smacked his lips several times. "I'm actually more thirsty than anything," he said in rapid succession. "You wouldn't happen to have any water or... some alcohol? I could really use some. They say drinking while you're dehydrated can make things worse. But..." He shrugged.

Ava splayed her arms. "Where would I carry it?" She replied, as cold as the air he wished was blowing in his face from an office air vent.

He gave her another once over. Neither her T-shirt nor shorts had any pockets large enough for a container. Nothing hung from her belt loops. She wore no backpack or purse, and her hands were as empty as his growling stomach.

"Satisfied?"

"Not really." He frowned.

"Now is the time to start getting used to it. And before you speak again, I'm going to remind you… we don't have time for all of this back and forth. Well, you don't have time for it."

He opened his mouth to speak.

"Shut. Up." Ava interjected. "I don't feel like going through the same thing with you as I did with the other six. Yes, the other six. Meaning you aren't the first, but you should be the last. Now, to clear up any confusion on what's going on with a slight explanation of how you have found yourself in this predicament." She pointed at his chest. "You're dead. How? I don't know and it doesn't matter."

The words hit him with the intensity of a heart attack. His chest tightened as his heart ping-ponged around in his ribcage. He ran through all five stages of grief in quick succession. His face morphed and contorted as his mind stumbled over each milestone.

"Good." She nodded. "Looks like you understood quicker than the other six. Two hundred points for you. Keep going in this direction and you might take the lead." Ava smirked.

Andre looked around at the vastness of the desert with its endless dunes and the clear blue sky above. His eyes strained as his vision swept by the bright star in the sky. Everywhere he looked was empty, except for the endless sand and that damned Sun.

"You're in hell," Ava said.

His head snapped back towards her.

She gave a slow nod. "That's right, hell. One level before the big chill. Where's all of the fire and pitchforks?" Ava quickly asked as if she read his mind. "It doesn't work that way and once again, that doesn't matter. You are here and you will be here, for an eternity. There's no escape for good behavior. There weren't any mistakes made by the management. No kind of grand promises, crying, denial, or any kind of apology that you can think of will free you from your sentencing."

He grabbed his left shoulder and dropped back, collapsing to his rear end. A puff of sand drifted up around him. The heat from the sand leeched through his cotton slacks.

"You will remain here, constantly walking through this intense heat, never to find shade or any liquids that will quench your ever-growing thirst. You will find no food for nourishment. You will grow tired and weak but stopping to relax will not relieve you from your hardships. Because if you do stop to rest your weary body, the Others will come for you, and they will find you." Ava stepped closer to him. "And when they do, you will wish you never had stopped. They will afflict pain on you that you've never experienced or could have ever imagined in your natural life."

He tried to cry but he could not. His face contorted into all of the correct positions; squinting eyes, furrowed brows, and frowning lips, but the tears would not come. All of the water that was stored in his body was wasted on the sweat that drained from his pores. The salty mixture stung as it passed over his abraded skin. The moisture that collected on his exposed skin only amplified the sun's rays. Baking his face and hands and turning his outfit into a personal sauna.

"Why are you telling me this?" He whispered, staring at the shifting sands between his legs.

"Because…" She walked up to him. Her shadow covered his body from head to toe, but her silhouette did not bring him even the slightest bit of relief from the heat. It was as if she was not there. "I have a proposition for you. Something that can—get you out of this hellhole."

He looked up, squinting from the light. Hope resurfaced on his Sun-beaten face.

"But it will cost you more than anything you have paid so far."

And just like that, hope was gone once again. Andre looked back down. "What do you mean?"

"I need a piece of you," Ava said. "A small piece. You won't miss it at all. But, once I start my plan, the Others will notice, and they will take a particular interest in you. They will hunt you down and torture you for your transgressions. But, with that pain comes your freedom. You'll simultaneously be making a sacrifice while being a sacrifice. After that, your time will be up, and you will move on from this place to live so much better. If there is such a thing in the afterlife."

The wind picked up, swirling around both of their figures, blowing particles of sand up into the air, clouding the sky. Ava stood in front of

Andre, tapping a toe in the soft sand, as he sat, mowing the proposition over.

"If I keep moving…" he finally spoke, "forever… I can avoid the Others."

She nodded. He did not look up to notice.

"And If I stop moving for too long, the Others will catch me and do horrible things."

She nodded again.

"But If I give you what you want, then-- no matter how fast I move, the Others will find me and catch me."

"That's true but—"

"You should keep looking. I'll take my chances."

"You will stop walking at some point. If not the heat or fatigue, the hallucinations will get you," Ava said.

He climbed to his feet, straightened out his tie, and dusted off his clothes. "Struggle until you can't anymore." Andre winked at Ava before stepping past her. He waved without turning back around.

Ava's eyebrows twisted up. *What an odd response.*

-1-
OLD FRIENDS

There she sat, as alone and on her own as she had ever been. Surrounded by music and patrons, Ava sat at a small round table, stuffing food into her mouth. Three full plates occupied parts of the table; loaded chili fries covered in nacho cheese and topped with onion rings, an assortment of boneless buffalo wings, honey garlic, ginger chili, and whiskey maple, somewhere in the range of fifty, and a bacon elk burger that previously matched the one she was finishing off at the moment.

Montanans trickled into the tavern throughout the hour. They greeted her with warm smiles, comments on her abundance of food, and her lack of companionship. In return, they received not a single word. She only gave a cold stare before returning to devouring her meal. Callousness has been one of her dominating traits for over a decade now, and tonight—she will need it more than ever.

Internal whispers hit her mind's ear, light as a feather, beckoning her to reconsider and change her plans; but she suppressed those voices. Ava was focused and determined. Swaying from the course was not an option. Headlong and straight into the storm was the only way she could get any lasting peace. Since climbing out of the Abyss, that storm has always been on the horizon; lurking, tracking.

Her five years of running had been long enough. *Everything will work out. It has to...* She stared at her food for a moment. The confidence silenced the doubtful whispers, but it was not enough to truly convince herself.

Exhaustion will break most people. The lack of sleep, the ever-changing environment, the absence of the familiar. They slow down, slip up, and make mistakes. Their goals fall apart in front of their eyes like an eroding cliff, cascading to the darkness below, dissolving like an apparition. Hope fades just as fast. That is when the bleakness of the situation takes over and they become an all-knowing prophet to fulfill their own prophecy. "Not me." She shook her head, reaffirming her position. "There is too much at stake. There's only one thing left to do," she whispered to herself.

Time passed, like it always does, and always will. During its passing, Ava continued to eat and drink, ordering double the helpings of almost everything on the menu. Her bottomless stomach provoked chatter amongst the other customers and caused the tall, scruffy barkeep to watch her like a hawk. His eyes only left her on a few occasions to mind the rest of the customers. Her extensive tab had surpassed the one-hundred-dollar mark more than two hours ago. Some of the non-locals who pass through this small town have been known to ditch their bills while pretending to use the washroom or saying that they forgot their wallet in their car. There was only one sheriff and five deputies in the area, which included three other towns that were much bigger and more populated. So, if a patron just so happens to skip paying their tap, there was most likely no real recourse for justice.

Fate came that evening, as it always does, like an unwelcome guest forcing its way into your life. As Ava was reaching the end of her copious amount of food, mere moments before dusk, two women, walked into the tavern just like everyone else, and to everyone else, they were just your average travelers, making a pit stop in their small sleepy town. But Ava knew, without the need of looking up-- she knew her time was almost up.

"Look who it is," the lead woman said. Her voice was high and full of excitement. Uninvited, the duo pulled up a couple of wooden chairs. They screeched as they slid across the ground. The woman on her left sat next to the table first. "What do we have here? Burger, wings, and chips? A right proper meal." The woman reached over and grabbed a loose fry from Ava's plate. "I do feel a bit peckish."

Ava glanced up, catching a glimpse of the woman to her left. Kismet Khatri—The mighty Urumi, sat with her head tilted to one side, taking small bites from the pilfered French fry.

Kismet Khatri was born in Tamil Nadu, India, a few miles from its southern tip. She spent her toddler years in that southern region before moving with her family north to Punjab to stay with her father's relatives. From what Ava was able to discover, Kismet did not spend much of her life in Punjab either. After her father's untimely death, Kismet's mother relocated her family once again. The final move was to south-east England, where Kismet would spend the bulk of her impressionable years. Kismet's family went from relative squalor to luxury with her mother's marriage to a wealthy British real estate investor.

Even though she was not quite a Londoner, it did not stop her from telling any and everybody the opposite. Whatever free time she had, she spent it in South London with the local roadmen at the grimiest estates. The danger, fashion, style, and slang drew her in like an oarless boat to a massive whirlpool. By the time Kismet had turned sixteen, she had escaped her strict family and took up permanent housing in the East End with low lives and societal rejects such as herself.

Kismet's leg bounced from her heel tapping on the wooden floor. Blue jeans fit tight around her long lean legs. Her chocolate aviator jacket's fat white fur lapels sat up high like the popped collar on a preppy frat boy. A large white crocheted beanie contained the majority of her ponytailed jet-black hair. Kismet rotated a silver ring on her thumb as she watched Ava.

"It's been a long time, Ava," the other woman said, standing by the second chair. Her mouth smiled but her eyes did not. "You haven't changed one bit. Not a day over twenty… two." Her husky voice sounded familiar. "How long has it been? Seven years? Eight?"

Rhea? Ava questioned herself. The possibility did not sit well with her. Ava looked up with hopeful eyes. She was eager to see the evidence of her poor judgment, only to be simultaneously shocked and disappointed. It was her. Rhea Kane. She was the walking, talking catalyst to this very predicament that Ava had found herself in.

She sat directly in front of Ava, with a smile as bright as the day they first met. Rhea looked almost exactly the same as she did back then too. She had the same pale, vampire-like skin. It was as if she barely spent thirty minutes a day in direct sunlight before rushing off to cover herself up. Rhea still dressed like a bohemian princess with a variety of thin, pattern-filled linens, died with muted earth tones.

A thick scarf with small tassels wrapped around her neck several times bulged under her chin. Her slender fingers had a collection of rings made from different metals; silver, gold, copper, palladium, and what looked to be brushed steel. Each ring had a different precious stone or crystal embedded in it. They were also etched with words, phrases, or symbols.

High-level Followers of the Abyss, Travelers, or even Initiates like Rhea typically would have at least one enchanted item that they wore for their most frequently used spells, hexes, or charms. The use of enchanted items helps the wearer to boost the power and longevity of the skill while cutting down on the preparation and endurance that might be needed to cast.

Ava noticed Rhea's hair. It was the one thing that resembled any indication of passed time. Her hair was shorter than Ava remembered. A lot shorter. Rhea's once long, shiny, burgundy hair was cut as low as a freshly shaved army recruit.

"Seven years, yeah? Long time to not chat, innit?" Kismet said.

Rhea nodded. "Just about. Did I ever tell you about us?" Rhea did not wait for Kismet's response. "Me and Ava were Greys together—remember that?"

Ava ate faster. She stripped pieces of meat off the buffalo wings, combined it with a few onion rings, and crammed the handful into her mouth. She barely chewed any of the food before swallowing the mouth full. Grease and small pieces of food clung to her mouth and chin.

Kismet grimaced at Ava's awful table manners. Her eyes shifted away to observe the rest of the room.

"We learned some of our first few charms and hexes together. Some were better than others," Rhea continued. "Remember this one?"

Rhea nodded towards a young man coming from the washroom. Ava turned her head in that direction.

"Damnum statera," Rhea whispered. She pointed at the hapless individual. His sneakers squeaked on the laminate as he seemingly stumbled over his own foot and collapsed to the floor. He tried his best to control his landing, but his outstretched arms were not strong enough to stop his momentum. His boyish-looking friends laughed hysterically at his perceived inability to hold his liquor. Two of them high-fived as if they were the perpetrators of some grand plan. The fallen young man clambered to his feet as soon as he was able, dusting himself off in the process.

Kismet smiled wide, exposing her sharp golden-capped canines. The tip of her tongue peeked out from between her front teeth. Ava on the other hand was not amused in the slightest. The days when she would relish in the misery and mishaps of others had been over for quite some time.

"When we started out," Rhea continued as if the incident she caused did not happen, "we were kind of inseparable. Like peanuts and cola." She gave Kismet's leg a quick tap with the back of her hand. "Or bangers and mash."

"You lot? More like fish and chips," Kismet said. She snatched up another French fry.

Rhea paid Kismet's comment no mind. "We did everything together. You name it, we did it." She looked at Kismet. "I mean everything. Isn't that right Ava?" Rhea smiled. "Sometimes, when we would drive through a college town, we would stay for a few days at the local motel and create all kinds of havoc on campus." Rhea snickered. "We would charm all of the guys there and turn the girls on one another… well, I would." Rhea laughed. "My darling Ava once convinced a guy from Utah who had, what was it, a few hundred hours on a bargain bin flight simulator in his mom's basement, he could pilot a commercial airplane." Rhea's cool blue eyes watched Ava as she recounted the story. "What was that boy's name?" She waited for the answer like a game show host. A little less than thirty seconds went by before she continued. "Let's call him… Jonesy."

His real name was Darius. Darius Crawford. Ava never forgot his name. He was one of the first to fall victim to their antics. Until then, their actions caused nothing but ruined relationships, lost property, and a few minor injuries for the people they encountered. Their lives might have been shaken up by their chance encounter with Ava and Rhea, but the victims would always part ways with their lives.

"Ava helped Jonesy get past security," Rhea said. "Ten minutes talking, and Jonesy was on one of those 757s. He went up and went right back down in a nearby field." Rhea mimicked the short flight and the crash with her hand. "One of the turbines broke off and crashed through a barn. Good ol' farmer John probably lost half of his livestock. She was decent at most things—but fraud… Ava was always good at faking and taking." Rhea's pleasant face vanished. Her gaze locked back on to Ava.

Ava stopped for a moment, soaking up all the tension in the air before continuing to eat. Her two interlopers continued to talk amongst themselves like gossiping teenagers.

"You two met before, Kizzy?" Rhea asked.

"I saw her about two or three years ago," Kismet said.

"Really?"

Kismet nodded with her eyebrows raised. "I was in the Boston area. Spot of tea and all that, yeah. Big tings brewing." She gave a half smile.

Rhea gave her a knowing glance.

"I spotted the bird coming out of some park. Can't recall the name," Kismet shook her head. "I've never been good with the names here. But I knew that face. How could I not?" Kismet winked at Ava. "I saw her, down the footway. She was carrying some proper baggage. Now that I think about it, it looked identical to the one she left in her room this morning."

Rhea pushed some of the used plates to the side and dropped the empty black canvas bag on the table. All of its pockets were unzipped.

"I called out to her," Kismet continued, "at least ten times, but she must not have heard me. She crossed a rotary—and then I lost her in the crowd crossing the zebra."

"Head down?"

"Like now," Kismet nodded, "minding her toes."

"That sounds like her." Rhea smiled. "She used to stare at the ground while she walked, completely oblivious to what was going on around her. She looked like she had lost her best friend. She was a sad thing." Rhea pouted. "From what she told me; she was completely different before—"

Ava looked up. Her eyes were as sharp as daggers. Rhea almost crossed a line they swore they never would. Personal history could be a particularly touchy subject amongst Followers of the Abyss. Information was a currency that could buy you plenty of things, including power over others. And who wants to be controlled by the strings of their past?

Kismet was unaware of what was going on, but she slowly realized, she did not know either woman as well as she had once believed. Kismet cleared her throat. "Enough with the pleasantries, yeah?"

"Agreed," Rhea said. She leaned back in the chair. "You already know why we're here. I'm sure of that," Rhea said. "History or not, we have a job to do. Where are you hiding them?"

Ava took three large gulps from her brass-colored plastic cup and belched, loud and obnoxious. Not a single ounce of concern or embarrassment was on her face. The rest of the patrons cared as little as she did. Their focus stayed with their companions and merriment. Ava ate the last forkful of fries and leaned back into the chair, wiping her hands and mouth with the stack of napkins. She tossed the used napkins on top of the empty plate.

"We're only here to collect, Ava. Nothing else," Rhea said. "All you need to do is give everything back. So, where are they?"

Ava did not speak, and her face did not betray her. Both her mind and body were in one accord. They would get no information from her, no matter how dark the night might turn out. Her lips were sealed, much like her fate.

"You don't want to talk. Huh? You have got nothing to say. Stubborn as usual," Rhea spat. "That's fine. But you will listen." Rhea's nose flared. "Nathan is coming."

Ava repeated the name under her breath. Her heart thumped. She hid her dread as well as she could. "I knew he would," Ava said matter-of-factly. "I imagined he would have been the first to show his face. I never would have guessed you."

Rhea looked away.

"Oi," Kismet said while jabbing a finger in Ava's direction. "Give us what you nicked, you muppet. You can't handle the both of us, mate," she insisted.

A couple of patrons looked around startled from the commotion that was building at Ava's table.

Ava cut her hard gaze to Kismet. "And I can't keep running either," she shot back. "This is where I stand. I'm not going anywhere."

"So dramatic," Kismet said with a smile.

"A stand?" Rhea laughed. "Come now, Ava. You've picked the wrong day for any of that."

Ava stayed silent. Her fingers drummed on the table, rhythmically. The thumping of her fingertips made a sound like a wild mustang galloping across the prairie, a sign of impatience and arrogance. Those were two emotional states that Rhea could not stand, even on a good day.

Rhea glared at Ava's hand for a brief second. "Either you give them to us or have them taken by us." She checked her oval-faced analog watch. The seconds ticked away. "There's a full moon tonight." She pointed towards the ceiling. The ducts, vents, and electrical cables, exposed like twisted worms in soaked soil, snaked along the I-beams. "You remember what that means?"

"There's too many people out tonight," Ava said while looking around the tavern. Most of the tables, booths, and bar stools were occupied with customers yammering away in the background, not noticing the tension that was building at Ava's table. Outside, people walked back and forth on the main street, chatting, or having a smoke. Saturdays had always been the Tavern's busiest day. "Someone will witness. I doubt the Abyss is willing to risk a war over me and a few misplaced items."

"If it comes down to it." Kismet shot back without missing a beat.

Rhea touched Kismet's shoulder with a calming hand. Kismet relaxed immediately. "It's a small-town Ava."

Ava looked at Rhea. "I still remember the rules."

"The rules?" Kismet scoffed. "The rules don't apply to you anymore."

"You have nowhere to run and nowhere to hide Ava. So, instead of going through this—standoff and wasting all of our time, give us back what you took," Rhea said.

"I'm not going to be touted around and tortured so you two can move up in the ranks," Ava said. Her hands slid towards the edge of the table.

"Ava—don't," Rhea demanded. "It doesn't have to go that far. We can keep this—civil." Her voice relaxed. "Just hand them over."

Ava's hands crept closer and closer to the edge of the round wooden table.

"Stop," Rhea shouted. "Keep your hands on the table."

Kismet licked across the edge of her top row of teeth as she smiled, brushing past golden caps that covered her canines. They twinkled in the dim tavern light.

The scruffy bartender who had been keeping a periodic eye on Ava throughout the night walked over to the table, small towel in hand. "Excuse me, ladies." He dried his hairy hands with the towel. "Is everything cool—over here?"

Ava smiled, her eyes never leaving Rhea's face. "Yes. We were just arguing over who would pay the check."

Erik McGowan

-2-
LUST

Rhea brushed over her short hair with both hands. Blond streaks followed her slender digits as they passed through her lengthening hair. After a couple of strokes, Rhea's hair stretched down to the back of her neck. She tucked some of the loose strands behind her ears. Rhea gave a modest smile and batted her eyes. Her irises shifted closer to an icy blue hue with each blink. She took off her shawl and draped it across her lap. "Hi."

The bartender's jaw and the small towel he was using to dry his hands collectively dropped to the floor. To his astonishment, Rhea Kane looked exactly like his first love from high school; Peggy Scott.

Peggy, who was sometimes affectionately called Ms. Piggy by her two best friends for her unyielding confidence and drive, was a rambunctious filly that shattered his heart two weeks before their junior prom. She dumped him in the middle of English 3 in front of his best friend for one of those letterman-jacket-wearing jocks, Tod or Thomas, or Terry. He could never quite remember. What did stay etched in his mind was the months that followed that day of devastation. He spent those months in a daze. He avoided school events like homecoming, the infamous high school mixers, and the once all-important junior prom. His outlook on life slipped with his grades.

"Peggy…" he said with every bit of longing that he held on to for all those years. His arms dropped down to his sides.

Rhea reached out with a dainty hand, leaving it in mid-air like a southern belle or a royal, offering their grace to a lowly commoner.

He grabbed up her hand like loose change, swinging it lightly. His thumb rubbed the smooth skin on the back of her hand. "You look… breathtaking," he said.

She smiled at the compliment, teasing her hair with her free hand. Kismet and Ava watched quietly like polite moviegoers during the exchange. The bartender was helpless under Rhea's influence and so was Ava. Charms, a favorite of Rhea Kane, can, if the caster is skilled enough, overpower all of the victim's senses, and stop the interjection of anyone who would try to compete with the caster's control. Charms like that can be particularly potent when used on a person by the sex they are most attracted to. Because of that, Ava was helpless in the situation. She could only watch and wait, not knowing what Rhea had planned for the poor bartender.

"Can you do me a favor?" Rhea asked with her head cocked to one side.

"I would do anything for you." He kissed the back of her hand before patting it.

"The girls and I would like to talk in private for a few minutes. Can you close up for us?"

"Of course," the bartender said without a hint of hesitation. "Of course." He kissed her hand one more time. "After that—I wanted to talk to you about us. I've been missing you some kind of fierce. And… I've been wanting to tell you for the past twenty years. I—"

Rhea gave a slow nod. "I understand. I really do," she said, snatching her hand back from his constricting grip. "But first… it's closing time."

He smiled with coffee-stained teeth.

Within five minutes, the bartender had shut down the tavern citing 'unforeseen personal issues' for the abrupt closing. The majority of the customers, which consisted of small groups of friends huddled around wooden tables or sandwiched in cramped booths, with the occasional couple who shared each other's space but not their presence while they stared blankly at their phones, left without putting up much of a fight. They said their goodbyes, wished him and his situation well, and funneled out of the front door, passing by the trio of women. Two of the regulars, Georgie and Matt, drunkenly argued with each other over their perceived 'real reasons' for the tavern's early closure as they stumbled out the front door.

Once the last customer had left and the front door was locked, the grizzled bartender moseyed his way back over to the table where his long-lost love sat. "I did as you asked Peggy." With his heart on his sleeve, he reached out for her hand, aching for her touch.

Rhea's gaze turned as cold as her ice-blue eyes. "We'll be talking in private." She waved him off. "Leave out the back and go home. It's late."

All of his exuberance drained from him at once. With shoulders slumped, he regretfully did as she commanded. The bartender slipped out the back door and into the night. He made his way home, just like she commanded, walking down route twenty-eight, studying the ground as he traveled, occasionally looking up to keep his bearings straight.

The three women sat in the stillness of the empty tavern for a couple of minutes. Kismet played with the silver ring on her thumb. Rhea sat with her arms and legs crossed.

Ava looked back and forth between the two of them until she could take no more. "We're alone now," Ava said.

"Yes, we are," Rhea agreed. She tapped Kismet's leg.

If Only For One Night

Kismet stood up, slipped off her leather jacket, folded it lengthwise, and placed it neatly on the nearby table. Her well-defined, dark brown arms hung out of her snug black tank top. Both arms were covered with all manner of tattoos, some words, some Hindi characters, some geometric patterns, and other different objects. Both tattooed sleeves were in black ink, which for the most part, could barely be seen because of her complexion, except for the tattoo of a woman on her left shoulder.

The woman's face was decorated with dark, squiggly lines that had a Morse code-like quality to them. They crossed the woman's cheeks, chin, and down her neck. The hair hung over her shoulders. Long bangs covered the top of her face like the brim of a hat, casting the eyes in a permanent shadow. The detail in the tattoo was astounding, life-like even. That tattoo was nothing like the others that crowded the rest of Kismet's arms. The other tattoos must have been inked by some amateur artist at a tattoo party or maybe created by some friend of hers who wanted to get their inking chops up by experimenting on actual skin. It was not the choice that Ava would have made, but 'to each their own' as they say.

Kismet walked over to the front door, unlocked the latch, turned its deadbolt, and opened the door. She stood there, holding it open for some yet-to-be-seen guest. In the distance, Ava could faintly hear the hum of an engine growing louder, drowning out the frequent chirping of insects that previously dominated the night's soundscape. Seconds later, the sound of that single engine doubled and then tripled. Ava looked over to Rhea who was now sporting a confident smirk.

"You've got about," Rhea looked down at her watch, "two minutes left."

Nothing but the growl of engines from speeding cars and the cool crisp mountain air came drifting in through the front door, but Ava did not dare take her eyes away from the gaping opening. Something was going to come through that door and Ava did not want any surprises. Her teeth clinched from the anticipation. Two minutes later, right on time as far as Rhea was concerned, the sound of tires grinding to a halt over loose gravel rushed through the door. Dozens of doors slammed shut with muffled thuds.

The Greys have arrived.

***

The Greys.

Some might call them inbetweeners or the lost or potentials or even cannon fodder. But what they truly are is something much simpler than any biased opinion. They are you and me. They are your family members. They are your friends and colleagues. They are the blue-collar workers and the single parents. They are the rich, the successful, and the homeless. They are the celebrity and the recluse. They are everyone, and in a sense, they are no one at the same time.

A Grey is ultimately someone who has not picked a side. They teeter on the edge of Light and the Abyss without ever knowing of their constant tightrope work. The slightest breeze or a couple of well-placed words could tip the scales and lead those individuals down a path to their place after death.

Most Greys never find out about this balancing act. They continue to live their lives the best way they know how. And then death comes, quick and silent. It snuffs out their life, and with a grim finger, points them to their destiny.

Some Greys, like the ones that just arrived at this small-town tavern, learned about the different sides from a 'reliable source' and made their choice. They chose to make the climb down to the Abyss. And from that moment on, their opinions, their wants, and their desires no longer mattered. Unless of course, those wants are in accordance with the Abyss and its master's wishes.

Ultimately, they are simple tools pining for a place in the levels of the Abyss. They try to prove themselves to their brethren and Initiates to garner power and respect within the Abyss and its rings.

***

"Lot of dodgy copper dripping from your gob, milady. Got you enough to break two bills?" Kismet walked back over to the table. "Twenty minutes love," she said, "two hundred Greys, plus. By that point, it won't matter what you have to say or who witnesses."

The Greys staggered into the tavern. The group ran the gamut of different sizes, shapes, and shades. Some were shaved with silky smooth baby faces, some with busy beards that puffed out like a lion's mane. Some had long hair and others were cut low. Some were stocky as an All-State wrestler. Others were hefty with beer guts and double chins. Some were clearly in their late forties and others looked like they had a remedial math class in the morning.

But with all the differences in appearance and backgrounds, what they all had in common was Rhea's mark. Each one of them was branded with a shiny pin, a patch, or some jewelry like a necklace or bracelet with a capital 'R'. Rhea always liked to flaunt the people she was in control of. Kismet watched Ava's eyes as she looked over each Grey that stepped through the door.

"One day I woke up and I was a cult leader." Rhea smiled. "Some say it's my personality, others…," Rhea said as she winked at one of the tall handsome Greys that stepped past her, smacking him on his backside, "They might say it's my looks."

The brooding Greys lined the walls near the entrance. Ava noticed their dull-looking eyes and their blank expressions. *Two hundred.* Ava's heart sank in an instant, terrified of the idea. Holding her own against sixty Greys plus the two of them would be a feat on its own, let alone a hundred forty additional Greys.

A voice spoke, clear as her own thoughts. "If only for one night," it said, cutting through all her doubt. It echoed like a distant memory. Hearing those words strengthened her resolve.

I can do this. She must do this. Ava's heart steadied. She took a deep breath. *Two hundred or two thousand, it is all the same.*

Ava grabbed the edge of the wooden table and in one quick motion, heaved it towards the two women.

"Kizzy," Rhea shouted.

Dishes and silverware crashed down to the floor. Food particles were catapulted across the room, spraying the cylindrical duct, nearby furniture, and a few of the Greys with small chunks of food. Rhea stumbled out of her chair as she tried to avoid the heavy table. She fell hard on the polished floor, bottom first, instead of face first like the young gentleman from earlier. She scrambled to get to her feet, but she was nowhere quick enough.

Hours earlier, while Ava waited for her first meal, she carved a small fire sigil with a seal surrounding it on the bottom of the table with a steak knife that came with the rest of her utensils. It was a simple sigil. Very easy to scribe without looking. That particular fire sigil is considered by many as more of a simple parlor trick than anything useful. Several seconds after the sigil is created, the marked area ignites with a small orange flame that burns for a few minutes and then dies out on its own. Adding the seal over the top of it holds the sigil's power in place until that seal is broken or released. In effect, it turns the fire sigil into a small pipe bomb.

With a light touch of her fingertip at the center of the seal, Ava released the energy that was stored in the sigil all at once. It caused a small explosion with enough force to blow a sizable hole around where the sigil once was. Wooden shrapnel shot out across the room, pelting the walls and a few of the nearby Greys. The spray of wood turned their faces, hands, and other exposed flesh into pincushions.

Rhea stopped climbing to her feet and opted to cover her face instead, protecting herself from the small pieces of shrapnel. The rest of the mangled table rocketed towards her. It slammed into her upper torso like a freight train. The force propelled Rhea's petite frame eight or nine feet across the tavern and into the wall just under its main window. Rhea was unconscious on impact. Her limp body crashed into the drywall, creating an imprint of her back. The bottom half of the window shattered. Fragments of the glass showered down onto her like a spring drizzle.

Kismet stood far enough to the side to avoid any real injuries from the wooden shrapnel or the table itself. She clambered to her feet with the help of some of the Greys.

A few of the Greys closest to Ava did not hesitate in the slightest once they saw Rhea's unconscious body. They immediately rushed in for an attack. Revenge would be theirs and Ava would pay dearly.

Normally, in most physical situations, a group attack with three or more assailants would always be regarded as the best option to dominate an opponent over a staggering, one-by-one assault. 'Overwhelm the victim with sheer numbers and they will easily fall, no matter how powerful they are—,' normally. There are a few instances, not many, but a few, where that sage advice is better skipped, and a full retreat is the best solution.

In this moment though, those attacking Greys had the right idea. Their problem was not in their numbers but in their inexperience and the absence of any sort of coordination. They bumped and stumbled into each other and the furniture in their path as they jockeyed for position. The Greys halfway defeated themselves before they could even reach Ava.

Ava backpedaled, cautiously maneuvering around the tables and chairs. She took potshots at anyone who came within range of her fists. Each punch was focused and directed, never missing her targets. Their heads violently shook from the strikes that connected with their temples, stubbled jaws, or the bridge of their nose. Their limp bodies crashed down onto overturned chairs or empty tables, unconscious or severely concussed. Her bare knuckles were wet with blood and saliva.

The five Greys that Ava crushed were quickly replaced by five more that funneled through the front door while she was fighting. Ava took a few more steps back to give herself some leeway. The new set of advancing Greys had apparently learned from their beaten brothers and took their time to approach. They pulled some of the unconscious bodies out of the way and kicked furniture to the side, opening the space for them and others to advance without any issues. Two of the brawnier Greys of the pack broke apart a wooden chair to use its legs as clubs. They laughed with confidence as they brandished their new weapons. They could not kill her, that right was solely reserved for any Travelers, Lords, or demons, but severe non-life-threatening injuries were not off the table.

The small group crept towards Ava, creating a semi-circle of muscle, anger, and wooden weapons. She backed up, inches from the stone wall at the back of the tavern. A golden framed painting hung from its rock face. The Civil War battle that was depicted in the brush strokes foretold the harsh realities of their upcoming fight.

The washroom's hallway was an option, but not a good one. Its walls could have constricted the flow of Greys even more than the constraint of the Tavern itself, but any further retreating would have come to an end quickly. There were no windows in the washrooms or any other rooms to escape from that hallway. The Greys would be able to wait her out until she was forced to come out of her hole.

With her back against the wall and no easy means of escape, the Greys launched themselves at her. Youth and inexperience tainted their plans like the previous set of Greys. Once again, they failed at working together. Their inefficiency ultimately caused their downfall. They swung wildly with furious strikes, much like a fame-hungry batter, who swings at every pitch with everything they got, in an attempt to get that game-changing home run.

She parried and dodged their strikes, biding her time. The Greys collided clumsily with each other as their attacks were redirected. Fatigue snuck up on them as they tried their damnedest to defeat her. Heavy breathing made way for aching legs, cramped shoulders, dry throats, and sweaty brows. The longer their assault went on, the further their goal drifted away. They dove in headfirst, trying to drown her with their numbers and brute strength, not knowing that they were the ones who were caught. They were stuck in a riptide, slowly being dragged out to the harsh sea where the real predators lived.

Ava saw her opening through their wobbling legs and sweat-drenched shirts. Each one of the Greys was quickly dispatched from the battlefield with a couple of lightning-fast punches and kicks. Their failure was yet another crushing blow to the morale of the Greys that lined the walls near the front door.

Ava dropped her hands to her sides and surveyed the room. Their wandering eyes betrayed them. Not a single Grey stood with an ounce of confidence. Their wills were broken like a derelict ship.

Through the crowd, Ava's eyes locked with Kismet. She stood near the center of the group, arms crossed, with a grin plastered on her face. Kismet was enjoying the exhibition. She had no loyalty to the Greys, with their patches, pins, and brandings. They would either earn their keep or they would not. Those slack-jawed Greys had nothing to teach her except stupidity. Kismet was far from being their Initiate and if it were up to her, none of those bumbling idiots would be seeking the Abyss. But, when you have hundreds to help collect a former high-level Traveler, there is no point in looking a gift horse in the mouth no matter how soft in the head it is.

Kismet stepped forward, shoving a few Greys to the side, openly challenging Ava.

The tavern was silent except for a few moans coming from some of the fallen Greys. Two of the closest Greys peeled themselves off the wall and dragged the unconscious or injured bodies out of Kismet's way. They watched Ava with suspicion as they collected the bodies and handed them off to others closer to the exit. Ava heard car doors slamming in the distance.

The alarm on Kismet's phone screamed to life, beeping two times before going silent. She did not bother checking it.

"Times up," Kismet said.

The tavern's back door creaked open. Ava shifted her head just enough to hear without taking her eyes off Kismet. The sounds of clanging metal and fallen objects came from the kitchen. More Greys, much more than before, streamed in from the kitchen and the front entrance. The already tight quarters became claustrophobic with the influx of goons. A few of the more excited Greys climbed over the bar to get in closer to the action. Others found an easier route over the booths that lined the opposite wall. A couple of Greys picked up bottles of liquor from the shelves behind the bar. Most of the Greys that entered the tavern from the kitchen were brandishing knives, pots, tenderizers, and any other cooking item that could be used as a weapon. They looked ready for a good old-fashioned, West Side Story rumble.

All of them were nothing but young hungry cubs, bright-eyed and bushy tailed. They tried their best to frighten Ava with their posturing and numbers but were completely oblivious to what they signed up for. Ava remembered those days, the rush, the excitement. The fact that you never knew what the next assignment would hold. There were some good times, for sure, but all-in-all, they were mostly hard. She felt sorry for them. They have gotten themselves into a life that will do nothing but drag them deeper into the Abyss, where their souls will reside for an eternity.

"Concentrate," a young voice whispered.

"They chose their side," another voice, more venomous than the last said.

The voices were right. They made their choice and she made hers. Pity and concern for those dozens of naive Greys vanished in a split second.

Kismet shook her head. "You must be daft." She gave a short laugh. "Rhea tried to warn you. And look what you did to her. Nothing but malarkey, yeah?" She nodded. "Nothing but rubbish?"

Ava's eyes shifted around the room, watching for any sudden movements. Several Greys played with their new weapons with devious grins, but none showed any sign of attack.

"There's no fraud to see over here sunshine." Kismet rotated her shoulders, giving them a quick warm-up. "And nowhere to run." She smiled with the tip of her tongue sticking between her teeth. "Ready?"

Erik McGowan

-3-
DUSK

Kismet Khatri, not waiting for Ava's response, pounced like a wild Bengal tiger. She dashed at Ava with blazing speed, swiping at Ava's face with a closed fist. The attack was so sudden that Ava barely had enough time to back away from the strike. The punch skimmed her cheek like a razor wielded by a skilled barber. Ava took a couple of steps to the side before bumping into the bar. A bar stool swiveled under her weight. One of the Greys behind the bar grabbed Ava's jacket by the collar and reached for her hair.

Ava fought the urge to retaliate against the handsy Grey. The immediate satisfaction she would have gotten from swelling the man's eye would have been a fatal error. Another punch from Kismet shot out fast towards Ava's face. Ava crouched, slipping out of the jacket's sleeves with arms raised. She dove past Kismet, rolling to her blindside. Kismet's fist made an impact with one of the Greys behind the bar. He was launched into the shelves behind him, knocking down the rest of the expensive top-shelf bottles, and collapsed into a heap. The unlucky fellow winced before passing out from the pain. Blood drained from the cuts he received from the broken bottles. The smell of cheap alcohol filled the tavern as quickly as the Grey collapsed on the floor.

Ava tried to sweep Kismet's back leg while her attention was elsewhere. Her tactic did not work in the slightest. Kismet lifted her foot out of the way without looking. In response, she sent a powerful mule kick hurling back at Ava. The kick came within an inch. It was close enough for Ava to see the traction design on the bottom of Kismet's trainers, a cluster of tiny trefoils. Ava squinted from the wind produced by the kick. She hopped back up to her feet, focused and ready for the next attack.

Kismet turned around and smiled. Her tongue licked across the edge of her upper teeth. Kismet stepped in with a barrage of attacks. This time Ava was well prepared. She hopped from side to side, bouncing on her toes. Ava bobbed and rolled her head from left to right, avoiding the punches by millimeters. Her short mohawked locs swayed with her movements. Though the two women were moving at terrifying speeds, both of them were breathing like they were sitting completely still. Neither one seemed to be getting tired from the exchange. Some of the Greys cheered as they watched the two women battle.

Kismet was a tremendous fighter. She was leagues ahead of any of the Travelers Ava had met in her past. Her nickname—The Urumi, seemed to be well-earned. But-- Kismet had some flaws and Ava was finally starting to see one.

Ava backed herself close to a fallen chair. She had been avoiding obstacles throughout their fight. Occasionally Ava would pull one or two of the fallen pieces of furniture in between them to slow down Kismet's pace. For the most part, it worked in Ava's favor, but this time Kismet aimed to use the obstruction to her advantage. She pressed forward with a quick thrust of her foot to Ava's chest. Ava stepped back, avoiding contact. Her heel bumped into the leg of the chair. Ava lost her footing and stumbled back a little, dropping her guard. Kismet smiled at her mishap, poised to strike. Her tongue, once again, peeked out from between her teeth.

And there it was, the opening that Ava was looking for was right in front of her. Ava recovered from her feint and quickly closed the distance. Kismet was fast. Even though the feint was well planned, and the distance Ava had to clear was under three feet, Kismet almost managed to avoid the attack. The uppercut landed on the tip of Kismet's chin. Her jaw snapped shut, quick as a bear trap. Kismet groaned, shuffling her feet as she backpedaled. Blood seeped from her mouth. The tip of her tongue which had stuck out like a snake tasting the air was now on the floor in front of them. Kismet swore into her cupped hand, blood leaked between her fingers. The muffled words did not sound like English. Maybe it was some curse in Punjabi, Tamil, or Hindi, Ava could not tell.

Kismet spat. A glob of blood splashed down on the tavern's floor. She wiped her hand across her tank top, leaving behind a ruby blood trail. The Greys did not wait for her approval or permission. Their Second was now injured and they would not let the degradation of command continue.

"Gravis aestus," Ava mumbled like a ventriloquist. Sloth activated in an instant. A ten-foot invisible barrier of torpidity wrapped itself around Ava like a protective bubble. The Greys came at her from all sides, passing through its boundaries without a hint of recognition. The longer they were enveloped in its field, the weaker and slower they grew.

Fifteen minutes had passed since the start of the all-out brawl and the verdict was all too clear. Ava had complete and utter control over the situation. Her initial fears of being overwhelmed or being dragged down by the sheer number of Greys turned out to be completely unfounded. The number of personnel was irrelevant to her skills. The gang of Greys was completely overwhelmed by the sheer chaos of the situation. Their hearts raced. Their minds careened. Many of the Greys stumbled into each other as they tried to force their way into the fray. Some of the fallen were trampled by the aggressive stampede.

They were outmatched in every category: fighting skills, strength, endurance, and speed. Sloth washed over them like a tremendous wave, weighing their bodies down with each crash of the surf. Their movements were like paddle boats to a jet ski or a child's tricycle to a super sport motorcycle. It was almost as if Ava was in two places at one time.

The tavern was packed, five men shy of the regulated capacity for the building, ninety-nine. The capacity sign was knocked down three minutes ago by the body of a thrown, unconscious Grey.

What could have been twenty or thirty minutes later, more of the horde of Greys came piling in through both the front door and kitchen. Some climbed down through the broken storefront, slipping past the shattered glass. The limited real estate dwindled down to nothing but inches, taking her upper hand down with it. She was fast, blindingly fast, but that speed meant nothing if she did not have the space to wield it. Ava, just like the rest of the combatants, struggled to get in clean and effective hits with any sort of power behind them. Her movements became too restricted for comfort.

There was an option. Though it was one that she planned on never having to use. But like most things, plans change when the times get drastic. Retreating to gain some much-needed elbow room quickly turned into the only option worth considering.

With a couple of quick hand gestures, the closest Greys were sucked toward her like they were near a small gravity well, and then, just as quickly, they were expelled backward from an explosion of smoke and a deep orange light. They collided with the rows of Greys that stood behind them, causing a cascading effect of tumbling Greys that almost reached the outskirts of the mob where Kismet stood, close to the front door. The smoke drifted through the tavern, lingering for a few moments in the confined space that Ava inhabited only a few seconds ago.

Coughing ensued. Two of the closer Greys collapsed to their knees, wheezing, and patting their chest. Fine powder puffed from their mouths like the opening of a fireplace while a chimney sweep is inside doing a thorough dusting. Other Greys waved the smoke from their faces, searching for Ava amongst the crowd. The few Greys that were knocked back, stood up with singed clothes and soot-covered faces and hands.

Kismet forced her way through the confused bunch. More than a few were bloody and bruised from the beating they received. Most of the Greys looked weary and haggard. Of those, some only stood out of fear of the consequences of failure. Others supported the defeated, giving them a body to lean on. Not a single Grey was prepared for what they had just faced.

Kismet made it to the center of the crowd. She sniffed the air like a bloodhound. Her nose flared with each deep breath. "Brimstone," she said.

The nearby Greys followed her lead and sniffed the air in almost the same fashion, looking more like a box full of hamsters than a dozen well-trained hunting dogs. They looked around at each other, surveying the room for clues. Each of them was as clueless as the other. No answers or hints could be found from their brethren. They turned back to Kismet, who was now kneeling, rubbing the black dust on the ground.

"She opened a bloody gate." She sprang back up. "She can't stay in the Abyss for long. What's nearby?"

"Nothing," one of the Greys said. He answered quickly without giving the question much thought.

"Just one single tavern on the street, yeah? A proper ghost town. But what's this I see?" Kismet parted the Red Sea of Greys again and walked to the front of the tavern by the shattered glass window. She waved the outspoken Grey over. He followed behind her like a loyal pup. She pointed across the street. "Bricks and mortar?" Kismet grabbed the young man by the back of his neck, pivoting his head so he could see the rest of the 'nothing' that was out there. "Think first. Tosser!" She pushed him away.

He stumbled into some nearby Greys. They also pushed him away much like Kismet did. The Grey fell to the ground from the force. His face looked as if he had something to say but he did not dare to speak.

Kismet licked her bloody lips as she thought. Her face tightened from the pain. "That git didn't get far."

Kismet looked toward the kitchen's double doors that were behind the bar. The crowd opened a hole for her to reach the back of the tavern. Kismet took her time opening the back door. Behind it was a ragged mesh storm door. "Follow me," she said to the closest Greys.

"The rest of you lot, right… go round front, yeah–and check High Street. Look everywhere."

***

Sewage.

The whole alley smelled of rotten food and tubs of weeks-old liquid fat. The large trash bin beside the tavern's backdoor was empty with its lids closed but the smell clung to its metal like burrs on wool clothing. A trash truck that parted with the trash several hours ago left a wet trail of putrid liquid that wrapped around the building to the alley on the side.

The Greys walked out into the night, one by one. Their adrenaline pumped, causing their extremities to twitch uncontrollably, but not Kismet. The Urumi did not look nervous, scared, or excited in the slightest. She was calm and focused. One of the Greys covered his nose once he reached the alley. He complained about the smell and the small dirty town.

His vocal complaints caught Kismet's attention. She spun around and approached the closest of the three.

"What?" He looked baffled.

She moved closer, looking up at his acne-scarred face, trying her best to stare into his eyes. "What do you see?" She grabbed him by the collar and yanked him down closer to her eye level. After seeing enough, she pushed him away. "You were charmed. Right before she opened the gate." She looked around at the rest of the group. "All you

If Only For One Night

lot," Kismet said while pointing at them, "have been charmed. Wherever you think we are, we aren't."

In a split second, Kismet was snatched away into the night. She was seemingly yanked by her neck and then disappeared into thin air. One moment she was there, the next, nothing but tall buildings, a couple of parked cars, and all the spoiled smells of rotten food. They were all baffled. The Greys crept around, looking for clues to where Kismet had disappeared. One called out her name, cupping his hands over his mouth as he yelled. A few checked behind the bin and down the alley that led to the front of the tavern. One of them glanced at the rooftops and the fire escape that clung to the opposite wall. Seven Greys paired up and walked further down the alley, away from the tavern. They checked side doors, sewer grates, and the Golden Shark tattoo parlor. Its window's LED sign glowed with the welcoming word, 'Open', but no one responded to their banging on the shop's metal door.

The two by the Golden Shark that were banging on the door, collapsed to the ground. The other five Greys that were searching nearby, stopped on a dime. They looked around as two more fell. Panic set in. They were being picked off with no indication of what was going on. Bodies toppled to the ground, left and right. The group of Greys dwindled down to slightly over two dozen before the onslaught stopped. Then came the sound of wrestling and then choking.

The air itself was steadily getting hotter by the second. Some of the Greys took off down the alley. A deep primal fear overrode their sense of duty and their trust in the collective.

"Save yourself." It is a thought that screams from the animal part of the mind, warning and driving an individual to act in a selfish manner to survive. The cohesiveness of their herd broke apart as the group followed that prehistoric command.

Being newcomers to the Abyss, Greys have a tendency to be skittish and those select few that followed Kismet out into the night were no different. They ran as fast as their feet would take them, in different directions, never looking back to see if they were still in the midst of danger or not. Some even ditched their medallions. By tossing the items to the side, those Greys discarded the physical evidence of their connection to their Initiate Rhea Kane, and the Abyss that held their future. At that moment, the terrifying invisible battle that loomed around them held more sway than the warning of impending doom that would surely come for them if they were to ever break their pact.

-4-
THE URUMI

Ava stepped out of the crackling Gate into a small washroom stall. The sink's mirror was foggy from the heat that came from its opening. The Traveler's star that was once seared on her wrist like a cowboy's branding, burned like it did the very first time she received it. The pain nagged at her mind for attention, but the sensation did not overwhelm it. She had felt that intense pain before, though it had been quite some time. Every single time Ava would travel through a Gate, down to the dark Abyss, or back to the Earth's plane, the star burned anew. Ava looked down at the marking. It stood out on her skin, red and inflamed. She rubbed across her raised skin to soothe the pain. Its design will continue to fade, making it barely recognizable, and lose the power it shared with its owner.

A Gate, like the one Ava had opened and traveled through, is one of the quickest ways for a Traveler to enter the eight rings of the Abyss. By crossing the boundary of the underworld that is attached to the Earth's plane by the hip, Ava, or any other Traveler, can cover long distances on Earth in the briefest of moments. But with every Gate opened, much like every bridge crossed, there was always a toll to pay. This time the price was the more exact location of her partially hidden presence. That closely kept secret she had been holding onto has now been thrown away with one instance of magic. Because of her trip through the Gate, more Agents of the Abyss would come tonight, and much sooner than she had originally planned for.

There was a thin rectangular window in the wall left of the sink and mirror, close to the ceiling. Ava peered through it, trying to get her bearings but from her angle, she could only see the night sky. Small clouds drifted by like a collection of inner tubes floating in a lazy river. The full Moon glowed, spreading its silver light to the immediate surroundings below.

Where am I? She did not know. Ava could think of at least four different buildings in the area with a washroom very similar to the one she was currently in. Two of those buildings were close to each other, near the middle of the town. From what she remembered, both were a few hundred feet from the main road and filled with excess supplies and tools. The other two were on opposite ends of Route 28. Her trip through the hastily created Gate was so quick that Ava did not believe she could have managed to travel that far. That fact alone eliminated one of those destinations in her mind. If it was that one that she believed could not have been the outcome of her travel, Ava would have arrived in the neighboring town of Red Glen, around twenty miles between her and her haven for the night.

Ava's trip through the Gate did not take her far enough to get to the doors of her salvation either. It was a structure that had stood tall defiantly against Father Time and Mother Nature for several decades. Its appearance was as decrepit and ragged as her past, but its bones were still good. And in the end, that is all you ever really need—resilience and support. With that, you could take on the world or several hundred Greys, one or two Travelers, and a dozen or so demons.

The factory was only a few miles away. But traveling for any longer through the Gate was not a credible option. Opening a Gate was not one of her best options to begin with. It was nothing more than an act of desperation from her urge to escape.

Her escapism, which she originally considered to be an extreme case of wanderlust, was an urge she had for most of her life and apparently a compulsion she still needed to break. But right now, was not the time to berate herself over her shortcomings. The night started on a bad foot and she would not allow it to continue down that same route. Once again, Ava made up her mind to stand and fight and clash against whoever or whatever may come. She wiped the mirror, exposing its reflective surface to her image.

If only for one night. The other voices in her head echoed her sediment. Each voice stood as resolute as her own. In the end, it was all she really needed to do; make it through the night and arrive at the factory, no matter what. After that, everything would be better for her and those other souls. Ava had to stay focused. She needed to stay driven.

Ava climbed the wooden staircase, stopped at the door, and listened for any noises. She emerged from the basement of the Visitor Center. The Visitor Center was one of the few buildings that was completed and maintained throughout the years. The tavern was a mainstay since the day it was created, so it never lacked general maintenance and traffic. Even though the Visitor Center had seen more boxelder bugs than people in the last two decades, whatever profits that were made were first allocated to the structure and its skeleton crew.

There were displays at regular intervals throughout the floor space filled with brochures and maps for things to do and some of the best restaurants in the nearby towns. Pictures with plaques lined the walls, arranged by decades and regions. Histories of how the towns in the area were founded and some of their famous inhabitants helped describe what it was like one hundred years ago through short quotes. A circular desk with the words 'Welcome' embossed on its front stood near the center of the building, facing the double-doored entrance. On its counter was a cup full of promotional pens and a stack of mini maps of the town, North Forks. Ava could not help herself from looking around at the historical monuments as she absentmindedly strolled to the exit.

The history that hung from the Visitor Center's walls sent Ava's mind back through her own past. Ava's thoughts skimmed over her little brother, the souls she had taken from the Abyss, and the freedom that would come with the morning's first light. Ava smiled to herself. It was the type of smile that stayed plastered on her face when she was younger. Happy little Avalee. That was long before the cloak of innocence and the freedom of youth was stripped away and replaced with the weight of the world.

That smile did not last like most things in her life. When you allow your mind to drift, it can go in any direction. Her thoughts shifted back to the souls she held, their torment, and the pain they all had to endure so far. What would be their reward for all eternity if she did not succeed? Her smile vanished as quickly as it came, turning her face hard and cold as the snowcapped mountain peaks that loomed in the distance.

The memory of her parents moved to the forefront of her mind. It was one of the few memories she could remember where she was not angry and spiteful.

After watching one too many horror movies, which always led young Ava to hide in her parents' bed for the night, her father sat her down for a talk. "There's nothing to be afraid of, it's just a movie. Movies can't hurt you."

She knew what he was hinting at. He wanted her to go to her own room and sleep in her own bed. Ava cried. She looked to her mother for support, but she always stood with her husband in life and parenting.

"A twelve-year-old is too old to sleep in the same bed with their parents," her mother said. She sat on the edge of the bed in a lavender nightgown with a matching silk robe. Her hair was full of pink hair curlers. A pair of golden studs that she received for Mother's Day two months ago were in her ears.

"You have to be strong and brave," her father said.

She did not want to do any of that. Ava wanted to be safe from the ghouls and goblins, or any of the swamp monsters that might come for her in the night. Her father was already big and strong and much braver than she would ever be. Ava knew he could protect her. That was all she really wanted. She wanted to be safely sandwiched between her parents in their large bed until the morning light came to scare off any would-be terrorizing monsters.

"It will be ok," her father said as he walked Ava to her room, his large hand massaging her scalp. "Be brave. There is nothing to be afraid of. Go to sleep and we will see you in the morning."

No matter how sincere he was with his words, they did not sit well with Ava. Her crying grew louder as they crossed the threshold to her bedroom. Thinking back on that moment over the last couple of years, Ava began to see through the eyes of an adult, just how tired they probably were. Her parents wanted to be alone with each other like they could before she was born. The two of them were either working, taking care of all of her needs, or trying to get some much-needed sleep.

"Can you be brave for me and your mother?" He wiped her face, drying some of the tears. He tucked her into bed. "There you go. Snug as a bug in a rug."

Ava whimpered through the process, but she did not put up a fight. No matter how much she wanted to stay with them, her dad's "snug as a bug" quote always brought a sense of security and warmth.

"Be brave little bug. If only for one night."

Morning came like it always did and just like her parents said, she was safe. Seven and a half months later, her baby brother Levi was born, prematurely.

During her long trip down memory lane, Ava had not physically traveled far at all. She stepped out into the world cautiously, looking down both ends of the street. The North Forks stone marker stood like a baby obelisk. Its base was chiseled with the town's founding date and the date the marker was placed. The blacktop that led to Route 28 turned to dirt once it reached the town's marker and continued that way throughout the North Forks' borders.

Across the street, which faced the north, was the old town district. The majority of those buildings were husks. Shabby wooden buildings dressed up with the stereotypical trappings of a pioneer's town look. The imagery did not fit with the historical facts of life in North Forks, but the wide-eyed tourist would never know the difference. They were too busy taking pictures in the prop jail cells and volunteering to be trapped in the two pillories, on either side of the town, for a few minutes.

Overlooking all of the old town was the two-story inn, Old Cider's, with its wraparound balcony. It stood out from the background of tall trees and black sky with its orange pastel façade and bone-white trimming. The inn was like a big orange and cream pop sitting on the top of Watchmen's hill. A hill that was supposedly named after the men who watched over North Forks' surroundings for unwelcomed outsiders at night, possible thieves, and the occasional bear that might wander in for an easy meal. 'Welcome' and 'See you soon' hung on the left and right columns that flanked the front door.

A mid-size HVAC unit whirled to life when it kicked on and sucked in the mountain air to regulate the temperature in the Visitor's Center. It was tucked between the Visitor's Center and another building. Ava used that gap to make her way south, toward the factory. On this side of the main road, most of the buildings were new. Those buildings included one of the supply depots that was camouflaged to look like a dry goods shop and the Tavern from which she started her day. That last thought did not cross her mind as she made her way to the back of the Visitor's Center.

In front of her, Ava could see the factory looming in the distance. It stood stiff and stoic, in the valley below, less than two hundred yards from one end of the North Forks River. She would be there soon to finally finish the night.

The squeak and snap of a door grabbed Ava's attention. She drew herself close to the nearby wall. Ava peered around the corner with a quick peek. Nothing. Ava looked again, this time taking her time to look around. Ava examined the roofs and windows of the nearby buildings. She saw no one. Not a single soul. It was puzzling.

With all of the Greys that had come to help apprehend her, she assumed she would have seen at the very least, a handful of Greys scouring the area. She leaned farther out from the safety of her wall as she continued to search, only stopping once she saw the opened wooden screen door.

Ava watched as Kismet Khatri led a pack of Greys outside. The screen door slammed behind them. They fanned out, looking in different directions for signs of their prey. Ava was too far away to hear anything they said clearly but she studied their movements. She crept over to the next building to get herself a little bit closer. Her body pressed tight against the wooden wall. After a couple of moments, Kismet turned and approached three of the lead Greys who were covered in soot and ash like the rest of the bunch. She invaded their personal space with a show of aggression and dominance, moving within inches of the shortest one. The top of Kismet's head barely reached his shoulder.

Ava slipped out from cover while Kismet was distracted. Luckily for Ava, Kismet somehow managed to take only the Greys that were the closest to Ava when she opened the Gate. Mere seconds before she leapt through the Gate, Ava conjured a simple fraud spell with her hands, to buy herself some time. It was the kind of spell that only worked on the person or persons who were looking directly at the creator when it was created.

Ava did not know the number of Greys that would be affected or how long the spell would last but since the tavern was so jammed packed, Ava knew that it would be more than a couple. Ava infused the fraud spell with memories of a different location to disorient whoever was caught in it. It seemed as though fortune had returned to smiling down upon her with its radiant glow.

Ava could tell from the way Kismet was looking at the Grey, she must have realized what had happened. She also knew that Kismet would try to break the spell immediately. The distraction gave Ava enough time to launch a surprise attack.

It was true that Kismet was not a factor in accomplishing her goal. Ava could have run at full speed down to the valley where the factory stood while Kismet was busy with the confused Greys, made her way to the top floor, and then… what? There were over six hours left before sunrise. She had to fight and if she did not remove Kismet from the battlefield now, she might have to face her at an inopportune moment.

'An unprepared army will become fragmented with the loss of its leadership.' The outcome of the tavern was proof of that.

Ava stalked Kismet like a lion who spotted its prey through tall grass. She crept with speed and guile, not bothering in the slightest to stay out of view of the pack of confused Greys. Once she got close enough, Ava cocked back her arm and let loose with her full might. Her clawed hand struck Kismet in the side of the neck. The force sent Kismet tumbling, end over end, across the small, graveled parking lot. The Greys did not react as they did in the tavern when they saw their Initiate blasted across the room before crashing into the wall unconscious. They looked as confused and concerned as they did a few minutes ago. Exactly the way Ava wanted them to be.

Kismet climbed to her feet, none worse for wear, laughing to herself. "You got me again. I should have known." Her large beanie lay crumpled on the ground. White dirt dusted her blood-spotted clothes and face. She smiled with her stump of a tongue and bloody teeth. Irritation and pain showed briefly in her eyes.

Out of nowhere, Ava felt a strong urge to duck. Her well-honed body screamed the warning and she listened to its urgency without question. She felt a heavy wind blow past the top of her head, ruffling a few of her locs. Ava took a sizable step back as she stood, getting some distance from whatever had attacked her.

The smiling Kismet with her long black hair fanned out over her shoulders vanished within a blink of an eye, while another Kismet stood at Ava's side. Once again, Ava's body told her to move and once again she followed its command. Ava stepped to the left with her right arm shielding the side of her head. The blow came from behind, connecting with her protective arm. Ava stumbled for a few steps from the force of the blow but luckily escaped any real injury.

This time, Ava did not wait to check around for the danger. Her bewilderment was not going to stop her from getting some distance. She used the momentum from the attack to help propel her into a defensive roll, pushing her far away from the attacker, whoever that might have been.

Ava stood up to see the Greys still looking around the area, talking amongst themselves. The group moved like mimes in a park, putting on a show for anyone willing to watch. Ava could tell they were still blind to what was going on, but she could not tell if they were beginning to hear all of the commotion.

To Ava's left was Kismet, her long black hair covered with dust, and beside her was Kismet, an almost exact mirrored image. One was an inch or so shorter with her tongue intact. Ava's brows tighten for a split second. *That's what my body was warning me about?* Ava was confused by what she was seeing but she knew she could not show it.

The Kismet on the right dissolved from view as the other approached. "You're going to pay for earlier." Kismet spat out a glob of blood. Her smile was marbled with streaks of blood.

Ava was a well-experienced Traveler of all seven rings of the Abyss. She had learned skills and techniques from a few of the Lords from those rings and had never seen duplication at that level before. Lust, Fraud, and other sin-fueled charms can confuse the senses and lead to the belief of almost anything, but both disciplines need extreme skill and preparation to physically affect the person held captive in their influence. Something like that would be considered a Demon-level skill and from all of the stories that Ava had heard about Kismet the Urumi, she was a prodigy in the violent arts and not much else.

Kismet dashed in, raining down blows with seemingly no regard for conserving energy. Her hands were as stiff as blades, but the rest of her movements were as fluid as a whip. She struck at Ava's eyes and upper joints. Each attack was explosive and precise, but Ava stayed nimble. She managed to dodge each attack while making sure to stay a hair's breadth out of range.

Kismet's muscles rippled with every strike. As Ava prepared for her counterattack, she examined Kismet's footwork and hand placements. "Every attack by your opponent gives the opportunity for a calculated counter." It was a lesson that was drilled into Ava by her Den Mother. So, she watched. Her eyes were like a sponge, absorbing everything that she saw.

As she studied Kismet's movements, Ava felt a nudge from behind. It was like a quick push from a friend who is trying to help you with your cold feet. Ava glanced over her shoulder. Kismet or the duplicate stood behind her with an extended arm and flat pointing fingers. They poked her back, right between her shoulder blades, barely missing her spinal cord. The stiff strike bumped her forward toward the other Kismet who stood in front of her smiling with her partial tongue.

So, they both can hit me. Unable to react fast enough, Ava received a stiff kick to the stomach. Ava tightened her abs to absorb some of the impact. The force launched her off her feet and back through what should have been a solid person. Ava hit the gravel with a hard thud. Her tailbone stung from the drop. Dust puffed up around her. Two nearby Greys looked in her direction, squinting.

Even though she took the brunt of the attack directly to the abdomen, it hurt more than she believed it should have. She stroked her flat stomach with her left hand, trying to release the tension. Kismet gingerly walked toward Ava, pushing away stray strands of hair from her damp brow. Kismet then sprang back into action with multiple kicks that pushed Ava back onto her heels.

Ava bumped into the set of Greys. They were still inspecting the spot where she landed less than a minute ago like two seasoned detectives trying to solve the case of the century. One of the kicks that was intended for Ava's neck collided with the hapless Grey who stood with his hand stroking his stubbled chin. He bounced into the other Grey like two billiard balls with an audible crack as their heads slammed into each other. The force toppled both men. They lay there, sprawled on the bumpy ground. The sight of her colleagues being incapacitated yet again by her misplaced attack did not slow Kismet down one bit. Kismet continued to dictate the pace of their brawl and Ava had no qualms with that. Ava could see the openings, but Kismet's speed and that mysterious double kept stopping her counters. Ava hoped that the aggressive nature of the Urumi would slip up again at some point or tire herself out as she gave chase.

The next ten minutes of exchanges had proven the falsehood of Ava's theory. Kismet was not getting tired. Her moves were still quick and fluid. They whipped at Ava like the Urumi she was so appropriately named after. Ava went from being barely brushed from an attack to getting hit harder and more often as time went on. Her forearms and shoulders stung from a few of the blows that connected with her guard.

Kismet was learning and adapting to Ava's defenses. Even though Ava still had plenty of energy left in her reserves, she could not fight with Kismet all night. The remaining Greys could break from her fraud spell at any moment and leap into the fray headfirst. The influx of combatants could cause enough of an interruption to give Ava back some semblance of control, but the scales could easily hang heavier in their favor. She also did not know if Kismet's ability could work with others, thereby doubling their forces.

Ava decided to push forward. She dodged to the outside of Kismet's punch and hurled her own to the side of her head. Her fist stopped halfway to her target. She was hooked like a fish at the elbow by the other Kismet. A sharp pain spread across the side of her face. An elbow collided with her left cheek, near her eye. Her eyes tightened from the pain.

The pain from Kismet's attacks was getting worse. Gluttony was running low. Ava swung back again and again as quickly as she could. Each whizzed at their targeted areas and was effectively blocked or deflected. The second Kismet, or was it the first, Ava could not figure it out, was protecting the other. Ava tried every tactic she had ever learned from her Den Mother, including the famed Dance of Death. The Dance of Death was an offensive routine made up of thirty-two attack sequences that ended with the opponent on the ground, dazed, awaiting their end by a powerful death blow. Normally used with a weapon, the Dance of Death, with some modifications, could still be performed with your bare hands.

The technique did not work. Nothing worked and Ava was getting more worn out by the minute.

Twenty more minutes of fighting passed, and Ava was nowhere closer to victory. No matter if it was a counter or a blindside attack, the Kismets were always prepared. She would either appear somewhere behind or beside Ava, stopping her attack, or blocking without seeing it coming. It was like Kismet was reading her mind.

That's not possible. There had to be something else, some trick. Sweat dripped down Ava's face. Her breathing was no longer calm. Her mind state was no longer relaxed. Ava lunged at Kismet. Scooping up some dust and gravel from the ground as she went. Ava flicked what she collected into Kismet's face. Kismet stumbled back from the surprise attack. She turned her head and wiped at her eyes.

The plan worked. While Kismet was blinded by the dust, Ava's time had come. That is when she noticed that the tattoo on Kismet's arm was smiling.

A voice spoke. It had the same accent as Kismet, but it was a younger sound. "Andha?"

"Yeah, I'm blind. Bloody dust in my eyes, innit?" Kismet said through gritted teeth.

Ava paused, caught off guard by the exchange. She could not see Kismet's face as she spoke. *Is she talking to herself? Does she have some kind of split personality?*

"It was all a trick," one of the souls said.

"Yeah. Nothing but a dirty trick," another voice chimed in.

Ava did not want to make any snap decisions and fall into a trap headfirst. *Did the tattoo just smile or was it like that all along?* Ava tried to think back to when she first saw the tattoo in the tavern, but she could not remember the specifics. She remembered it being on her arm with the long black hair covering up some of its face and the markings but...

"Handle it, will you?" Kismet said.

"Khushee se. Tumhaaree Aankhen, tumhaaree dhaal," the disembodied voice said.

From the shadow that ran deep across the tattooed woman's face, its eyes glowed like two pen-sized spotlights. Ava had seen enough.

She did not know what was going on, but she needed to win first and then ask questions later.

Ava unleashed a fury of attacks. High and low, kicks and punches. They were hurled at Kismet from different directions and varying speeds. To Ava's surprise, each attack was either dodged or deflected once again. She was getting frustrated and very concerned. This fight has been going on far too long and Ava did not feel like she was making any progress whatsoever. The uppercut from earlier must have been a fluke. Ava was not really on Kismet's level. She was a prodigy, a protégé of violence.

"We can bring her down to you," one voice said, echoing through Ava's head.

"Yes. Don't you want her power?" Another voice chimed in. "We can take it for you. We can take it all."

The voices were right. She could strip Kismet of whatever power she might possess. Ava would just have to grab her, hold on, and let Envy and Greed do the rest.

Kismet peeked through squinting, bloodshot eyes. She wiped her face a couple more times with the back of her hand and tank top. "We see all," Kismet said.

"Ham sab dekhate hai," the disembodied voice said, slightly delayed like an echo.

"And you've missed your chance," Kismet continued.

"Apana mauka ganva diya," the voice echoed.

The tattoo bared its teeth before Its beet-red tongue slipped out of its mouth, long and pointy. Kismet mimicked the motion with her clipped tongue. Her golden fangs glinted from the moonlight. Kismet, the living Urumi, rushed in with new vigor.

"Demolio," Ava said in a light voice and rushed in as well.

Kismet launched a quick one-two-punch combination. A snappy jab to slow Ava down and then a powerful straight right. Ava bobbed under the jab and sprang forward in the middle of Kismet's second punch. Throughout the night, Ava had been trying to keep her distance from Kismet and Kismet had noticed. So, when Ava went for a takedown, it caught Kismet completely by surprise.

Ava scooped up her legs and with a sharp twisting motion, she slung Kismet to the ground. Kismet stuck out her arm to slow her fall and absorb some of the impact. The force knocked some of the air out of her lungs. Kismet grunted. Ava grabbed Kismet's left arm in a vice-like grip.

Kismet noticed something was wrong but could not put her finger on it. "Get off me," she shouted and kicked at Ava. The kick connected with Ava's shoulder. The force from the kick loosened Ava's grip enough for Kismet to break it completely with a quick yank.

Ava winced from the pain. She was only able to hold on for forty seconds. *Was it enough?*

Both women climbed to their feet. Kismet looked wearied and worried. She sneered and then summoned the double. Both attacked

Ava with a pincher tactic, striking from diagonal angles. Ava's kick reached Kismet first, connecting with the side of her face.

She's slower. Ava put up her arms and braced for the impact of the double's hook. It passed through her like a harmless apparition. Kismet held the side of her face, eyes wide. Ava grinned.

Kismet composed herself and then threw a couple more punches. Ava countered each with a punch of her own. Kismet's body and head rocked back and forth from the blows.

With every blow, Kismet slowed even more. Her eyes wandered like a parent in search of a lost child. "Siya?"

Ava's punch crashed into her ribs. She stumbled to the side. Her face filled with agony. The tattoo of the woman on her arm, Siya, Ava presumed, had faded slightly into Kismet's skin. Its eyes glowed no more. The shadow was back, covering the face. Ava kicked Kismet in the back of the leg toppling her. Kismet fell to one knee, scraping it in the process. Ava's next hit landed across Kismet's jaw, knocking her to her back.

"Siya..." The name came out slurred. "Help me." Kismet's head wobbled like a boxer on its way to the land of the unconscious. She strained to get back up.

Ava closed her eyes, tilted her head back, and sucked in the cool mountain air. It felt great to sit still for a moment. She was relieved. The fight was finally over, the Grey's were still as lost as ever, and she had plenty of time to reach the factory before dawn with most of the souls still intact. *A few more hours left and…*

Ava's thought was cut off. Her eyes sprang open from the sound of shuffling feet. It was Kismet with one last-ditch effort to finish off Ava. Ava saw the haymaker coming. Kismet was now moving as slowly as the Greys Ava had fought in the tavern more than an hour ago. Ava ducked the punch with ease, slipped behind Kismet, and locked in a rear chokehold like an expert pro wrestler.

Kismet desperately grabbed Ava's arms, trying her best to pry them off. She pulled at Ava's forearm and slapped at her elbow, but none of her attempts worked. She was tired and she was stuck. The chokehold was nice and tight. Kismet continued to struggle with no success. Ava pushed the side of her hip into Kismet's lower back and pulled at her neck in the opposite direction, lifting Kismet off the ground. Kismet's legs kicked as she felt her body elevating and the choke hold tightening.

She held on to Ava's arm with a fierce grip, trying to support her weight and get her body up high enough so she could get in a couple of quick breaths, but now she was too weak. The long fight and the contact with Envy drained most of her strength. The veins at her temples bulged as she kicked wildly at Ava's legs. Most of those kicks struck nothing but air. The few that landed only convinced Ava to tighten her chokehold like an anaconda wrapping around its prey. The kicks slowed for a moment as Kismet seemed to finally succumb to the lack of oxygen. Her hands loosened as her head drifted down.

A few seconds later, Kismet burst back to life with swinging elbows and clawing motions. Her fingers raked across Ava's arm, leaving trails of red but her fingernails could not break the skin.

If it were Rhea Kane in her grasp instead of Kismet raking at her skin, blood would have been spilled. Rhea's nails would have ripped through Ava's skin as easily as any well-sharpened knife. Even though most of Kismet's attacks did hurt like before, more from the kicks and the occasional elbow than anything else, her attempts to set herself free were not enough to deter Ava from loosening her hold.

Ava held on tight, making sure to keep Kismet in the air where she would not have any leverage. Kismet was much heavier than Ava would have suspected. Even though Kismet had more muscle mass, she was nowhere close to being double her size, and Ava was two inches taller. It felt like she was lifting two people. Her back started to ache from the weight.

Another elbow came flying in Ava's direction. She tucked her head further behind Kismet's back, away from her elbow's range. And with that last bit of effort, Kismet's movements stopped and her grip on Ava's arm released for the second time. Her arms fell limp to her sides. Ava, not to be tricked again by fake exhaustion, waited another second or two, just to be sure, and then released her. Kismet fell hard to her knees and then tipped over to the side. She lay there, mouth gaped open, eyes closed. The tattoo of the young Indian woman on her arm was now barely visible. The tattoo's head was tilted, and its mouth hung open like its owner.

With Kismet finally down, Ava could now focus on what was going on around her. Sweat trickled down her face. She wiped her brow with her palm and wiped the excess moisture on her dusty pants. She felt hot. Not exercise hot, but middle of the day, baking from the sun hot. Throughout the scuffle, Ava did not notice the heat that was building up in the area. The once cool fall night now felt like the Mojave during the day. Ava looked around.

A few of the Greys were still scattered about her surroundings, still bewildered by the recent events. She thought about eliminating them before they could come back to their senses but changed her mind since that action might be a waste of energy. She concluded that she would be better off moving on to what she was here for. Capturing every single pawn would not win her the game. Ava turned to walk away.

Ava heard a light crackling to her right. The noise resembled distant thunder or the sound of burning logs. The unmistakable smell of brimstone swept past her nose.

Erik McGowan

-5-
LORD OF VIOLENCE

Ava leapt away from the opening Gate like a frightened cat. A single arm reached out of the rift, barely missing her as she jumped. She spun in midair, landing in a fighting stance, ready to face the oncoming danger. Flames exploded out through the gaping hole like a jet engine. The heat was tremendous. Ava shielded her face from the intense heat. She took a couple of steps back. The flames danced around the edges of the oval opening. A few dripped from its edges onto the cool ground like hot wax from a tilted candle. The flames did not spread. They clumped together on the patchy grass like morning dew. The thin, dry blades of grass twisted, and curled, blackening from the heat.

The view on the other side of the gate was a bleak picture. Crooked and gnarled trees reached up to the dark sky. The faces that were embedded into the thick bark frowned like a big tent clown and cried out for mercy. Harpies pecked at their wooden skin and occasionally snapped off their branches. Ava remembered that place well. It was the realm of violence, which could only mean one thing. She swallowed hard.

A tall man stepped out of the Gate; youthful, slender, confident. The Gate slammed shut behind him with a gust of wind and a puff of soot. He approached Ava, one step at a time. Nathan the Cursed. Seeing his face, Ava's stomach immediately felt queasy. Her intestines squirmed like a bucket of mealworms. Throughout her years as Traveler and her time spent traversing through the various rings of the Abyss, Ava had only seen him a handful of times. She only saw him at a distance, but she could always feel his intensity.

Those few sightings and the stories that proceeded and followed had a strong lingering effect on her. Ava began to have vivid dreams of the Lord of Violence. He would come strolling into her dream, seemingly out of nowhere, speak some cryptic words, and then disappear as quickly as he came.

Sometimes he would watch her from a distance. She could feel his eyes on her as she went through her dream. After every single dream that his presence invaded, Ava would wake up drenched in sweat with the sheets sticking to her body. Ava was afraid of him, even when she slept. She could not escape the feeling. And now she would have to truly face him for the first time.

On the ground between Nathan the Cursed and Ava, kneeled a dazed Kismet. She held her face in one hand. A single eye peered through the gap between her fingers. Parts of her neck and tank top were covered in blood. When she fell from Ava's chokehold, Kismet landed on a few pieces of broken glass that punctured her skin. Her breathing was heavy and labored but steady. Her back arched like a drawn bow with each inhale. Through that one eye, Kismet could finally see through Ava's facade and relatively blank face. Fear. Terror. Kismet could read it all through Ava's dark brown eyes.

Kismet's legs wobbled as she tried to stand using her unoccupied hand for support. After making it halfway up, she fell back down to the graveled ground, catching her weight with her hands and knees before collapsing all the way again. Her jaw clenched from the jabbing pain of the marble-sized rocks. Kismet looked up at Nathan with pleading eyes. She reached out with a shaky hand.

Ignoring her motion, Nathan stepped over her body as if she were a log or some large rock in his path. Kismet turned her head up to the night sky, letting out a bellow full of anger and fury. The howl bounced off all the buildings nearby. It shook the windows and terrified the birds that were perched on the powerlines. The birds took flight. Panic-stricken, they flew deeper into the surrounding woods.

Intense heat radiated off Nathan in waves. The air around him wiggled, warping the surroundings, and distorting the light rays behind him. The buildings, the ground, the people, and even the distant stars seemed to tremble in his wake.

The heat was too much for Kismet to bear in her weakened state. She passed out again, collapsing face-first with a muffled thud. The ground under Kismet split open like a fissure, swallowing her whole. Once Kismet's unconscious body fell through the Gate, it sealed itself up immediately. The soot that remained was the only evidence left to mark Kismet's departure.

The Greys, the very few that remained, wisely gave Nathan a wide birth. The heat would dry them out and turn them into human jerky or scold their throats and lungs in a couple of heartbeats. Even at the distance they evaded to a few were still drenched in sweat. Their eyes were as dry as deserts, making it hard for them to watch the inevitable showdown. The closest Grey tried to shield his face from the heat with his bare hand. His palm quickly turned bright red before blistering. The decorative copper band around his wrist he got a few years back, which was supposed to help with his carpal tunnel, cooked his skin like a hot skillet. He screamed as he held his arm in pain. His brethren acknowledged his pain with gawking, but none moved close to help. He made a mistake, and he was now on his own. The smell of burnt hair and a hint of bacon tip-toed through the air. A few grimaced from the smell.

Greys in general are not equipped to handle temperatures anywhere close to Hellfire. Travelers, some Initiates, and other followers of the Abyss are different. They earned their safe passage through their deeds for the Abyss. Each Traveler, such as Ava or Kismet, is granted immunity to each of the rings' basic environmental dangers such as the gale winds that would otherwise bash a person against the jagged rocks covering the ring of Lust, the intense dry heat of the barren, endless desert, and the Hellfire that is used to cook its victims in their stone coffins. That immunity allowed Travelers to traverse each level freely. That way they could participate in the torture of lost souls or learn from the Cursed that controlled each of the rings. Because of that, the initial heat did not affect Ava in the same way.

Unlike Kismet, when Ava was still dedicated to the Abyss and everything within it, she was granted access to all of the rings that descended to the very deep. All of them except for the throne room, the massive room hollowed out from obsidian with basalt stalactites and stalagmites. That was where their master, from before and until eternity, perched.

As Ava's branding faded, the eight-pointed star that was once seared on the inside of her wrist, so did her protections. She could handle more extreme temperatures than normal, but Ava and Nathan knew that it would not matter once the Cursed decided to go on the attack. Ava glanced up at the sky. Thousands of stars and planets twinkled in the blackness.

The moon is almost at its apex. The closer the full moon drew to its full height, the weaker the veil between the two realities would be. Which in turn would allow more types of demons to join in on the hunt to collect her and the souls she had stolen. Ava glanced at the large factory a few miles away down in the valley. Those old bones would soon be her haven for the rest of the night. She just had to get away from Nathan and the last remaining Greys. Then and only then would she be safe.

Nathan continued his march forward. Nearby blades of grass that defiantly breached the graveled parking lot, sizzled and then curled as he stepped by. Ava followed his tempo, stepping back as he approached. Inevitability had come for her. She knew it and he knew it. His presence was always factored in, but that fact terrified her more than ever now that he was there in the flesh. There was no time for her to conjure up a spell, scribe a glyph, or create a seal to combat his flames.

Why did he have to show up so early? Ava needed a plan. Her mind sifted through her options like a prospector searching for those few golden nuggets. Some of her ideas shined like golden flakes, but with a little extra scrutiny, they all turned out to be nothing but fool's gold. He was dangerous. One simple mistake and that would be the last one she would ever make.

The fear that filtered through her brain and sent adrenaline coursing through her veins was not about his size or strength, even though he was well above average in both categories. It was because of the types of skills he had, the spells he could perform, and how he could do them. Nathan had always been well known for his immense flames, gifted to him from the depths of the Abyss where he has traversed and reigned. He did not need enchantments, seals, or complicated spells like a mere Traveler. Nathan the Cursed controlled and produced Hellfire with his thoughts and simple gestures of his hands.

His fighting skills were also in a league of their own. Ava knew she could not go toe to toe with him for any lengthy period of time. He was the Cursed. Nathan was the reigning alpha of the Ring of Violence.

For the last two centuries, there has been an uneasy truce between the Abyss and LIGHT, but when the war was at some of its most intense moments, Nathan was there. He was on the front lines, incinerating everything in his path. He was a walking, talking, wrecking ball; a Lord of Violence, molded to fight. Mayhem excited him, much like everyone else who has ever vied for his position. However, his thirst for violence transcended all except for the other Cursed beings on the other six rings.

Ava had never heard of him becoming weak or getting tired. He had never lost his balance amid a battle or hesitated to strike when the opportunity presented itself. Nathan was fast, ferocious, and cunning. Over the years, several of his lessers tried to gain his secrets to usurp him. Some emboldened Travelers and curious Initiates pestered him with questions about his methods. Others tried their best to stalk him through his realm, watching from a distance, hoping to catch Nathan in the act of some kind of preparation. But, as time went on, all that pursued his knowledge either gave up empty-handed or had their souls collected by him and placed on one of the Abyss's rings for all eternity. Some knowledge comes with a price that can be too costly.

The more Ava thought of Nathan and their upcoming showdown, the more she got nervous. But there was nothing else she could do. Nathan was right there, looming in front of her. His hands glowed from the intensity of the Hellfire. *This whole night was a mistake.* Her mind quickly went to failure.

The Greys did not move or try to seize their opportunity to injure a distracted Ava. "Alphas eat first." That was one of the cardinal rules of the wild and everyone who climbed down through the Abyss was nothing but animals. Their possible glory was all gone, snatched away by the bigger, stronger predator. There would be nothing left for them except the possibility of scraps and the ability to look back at this moment in their insignificant lives, months, or years from now, and say to themselves or others, "I was there when Nathan the Cursed caught up with Ava the Fraud."

Nathan was close now. His proximity interrupted her thoughts. So, she reacted with sheer instinct. Ava struck with a flurry of punches and kicks. Each one was thrown with tremendous speed. They zipped through the air like aggressive wasps. But to her disappointment and dismay, not a single attack connected with their intended target. Ava doubled her efforts and focused her mind on nothing but the task at hand. Her mind's eye saw what she needed to do before she did it. She saw herself hitting him across the face and then kicking him at the side of his knee. *I will not only hit him. I will hit through him.* After her mind's image, it was her body's turn for the physical part. She followed the scenario to the last letter, striking with all her might.

Again, Ava's strikes missed their target. Nathan continued to walk forward as if she was not putting up a fight at all. Ava's brow pulled together as tight as a coin purse with a drawstring. *Something should have hit.* She tried repeatedly, but she could not reach him. *Why? Why am I not hitting him?* He was so close. He was close enough for Ava to see every single vein that traversed his bloodshot eyes and the dozen or so black hairs that poked through at odd angles of his otherwise smooth face. He was close enough to wrap his long muscular arms around her in a tight back-breaking bear hug and then engulf her in Hellfire, and yet, Nathan kept walking forward.

The air between them wiggled like a bed of worms or a pile of interwoven snakes during the peak of their mating season. Ava's face dripped from the heat. She wiped her wrinkled brow, flicking the oily liquid to the ground. Nathan continued his march. Her heart felt like it was trying to free itself from her chest and escape the dire situation without her. Her mind was back to being jumbled as she attempted to make sense of it all. Her legs twitched with each one of his steps. In those fleeting seconds, while Ava corralled her nerves, she finally realized the truth of the situation; it was her legs all along. Her legs had been betraying her. With every attack she had launched at Nathan and with every step he took forward, Ava's terrified legs retreated, inch by inch. They kept her safe and out of Nathan's reach, but that safety also eliminated her ability to attack.

Ava gathered up all the courage she had left and stood her ground, planting her feet. Her body pleaded and even begged for her to run away or at the very least get some distance away from him, but she did not move. Ava waited for Nathan to get as close as possible. He needed to be close enough that he felt comfortable to attack and then Ava would counter the advancing brute like a limber matador.

He took the bait and rushed at her like a raging bull. With one hand extended, he tried to seize her shoulder or neck to hold her in place. Ava swatted his hand away at the wrist with a quick backhand, which in turn exposed his center mass for a counterattack. Ava struck hard, fast, and with the utmost precision. Her open palm slammed into his square chin, forcing his cold eyes to admire the stars. She felt a jolt of energy stream down her arm to her chest. Nathan staggered back a couple of steps, kicking up loose rocks.

The spectating Greys' jaws collectively dropped. They were watching something that, a moment prior, would have been an impossibility. Ava was striking the Lord of Violence and pushing him back with every hit.

She continued with a barrage of attacks as he stumbled back from each of her blows. Ava's attacks came in high and low. She utilized randomized patterns to avoid any possible counters. With each open palm strike, her body cooled, her mind eased, her heart rate slowed, and her strength surged. Nathan swatted at her with his hulking arms in between some of her combinations. Each swing ultimately missed while he continued to get hit by more blows that increased in strength and speed. The punches, kicks, and elbows that initially nudged his body in different directions were now driving him backward a few steps at a time with each hit.

I'm doing it. With each hit Greed and Envy sapped Nathan's strength, endurance, and stamina, transferring all of it into Ava. Ava's confidence grew as quickly as her newfound power. She could hear his grunts of pain. She could feel his body weakening. The bright blue blaze that once covered his hands had dwindled down to the intensity of a matchstick's flame. *A few more hits*, she thought as she continued her onslaught. *Just a few more.* A smile crept to her face as she beat his body into submission. He was just a legend, nothing more. Without his Hellfire, he was nothing. Her smile grew wider with each hit and each passing minute. Ava's fist slammed into his flesh. His body curled and twisted from the impact. Nathan struggled to find balance as he staggered like a drunkard. She had forced him back over thirty feet before she decided to go for the final blow.

Ava's arm stopped in mid-swing. Something felt wrong. Her body was once again urging her, almost pleading for her to back away from the fiery demon. She tried her best to ignore the messages that flowed through every cell in her body and forced its message up her spine to her brain, but the noise would not turn off. She looked at Nathan. His body stood frozen in place where her last body blow left him; doubled over with his arms wrapped around his stomach and his mouth gaped. A string of saliva hung from his thin lips. Something was definitely wrong. Her mind and body finally agreed. Ava took a few quick steps back with her guard still up.

Nathan tilted his head ever so slightly, just enough to see her backing away. He slowly closed his mouth and stood back up to his full height. Nathan's fist tightened to concrete blocks. His jaw clenched and within milliseconds, Nathan the Cursed was mere inches from her. Ava tried her best to defend against his attacks using the same strategy as before, repelling his strikes with quick swipes and then countering with devastating blows. This time, however, he was too powerful. She slapped at his incoming wrist, but the force and speed behind his swing penetrated her defenses and sent her tumbling to the ground. Her mind swam from the impact.

Even with all the energy Ava managed to sap from Nathan the Cursed with the help of Greed and Envy, all of that accumulated power never reached what remained within him. Nathan's power was a mountainous terrain several miles above sea level, scraping the clouds, and Ava was at the bottom of the Mariana Trench, struggling to reach his base. She thought she was rising higher and higher with every sip from his well, but in reality, she had yet to breach the surface of the water. Ava looked up at him, eyes wide, full of dread. She was outmatched and outclassed, with no real options but defeat.

Nathan raised his mighty hands, extending them towards her. The air between them once again wiggled and shook, distorting the light that passed through its turbulence. His hands burst into blue-white flames, baking the air. Columns of flames leapt from his hands like flamethrowers. Ava climbed to her feet in a split second. Palms out, she interlaced her hands creating a diamond shape. A bubble shield appeared around her body, protecting her from the incoming inferno. The blue blaze crashed into the protective bubble and bounced off its translucent golden coating. Some of the flames splashed to the ground around her, gathering into clumps. Other chunks of flames were launched into the air, landing on nearby roofs, melted sidings, and warped metal gutters.

Ava turned her face away from the intensity of the light and heat that came with the scorching fire. Her palms ached from the heat. The flames that emanated from Nathan's hands switched from a steady stream to quick bursts of heat and concussive force. Ava's arms jerked from the impacts, pushing them ever closer to her body, which in turn shrank her protective shield. She tried her best to stand but the force and heat from his Hellfire was too great. The pain in her hands from the smoldering was getting worse by the second, but she had no other options. Ava's shield was the safest place for her at the moment, but it took almost everything she had to keep it up.

Nathan moved forward methodically as he poured on the heat. The flames that bounced off Ava's shield leapt further away as he approached, scorching everything they touched. The building behind Ava, a replica of the town's old dry goods store, except for its modern central air system and lighting was one of the first to become completely engulfed. Wires melted, light bulbs exploded, and the satellite dish on the ground that pointed off into the blackness of space, blackened and sparked.

Heavy noxious smoke hugged the ground like a morning fog, threatening to creep into Ava's bubble and suffocate her once there was a single crack in her defenses. The heat that soaked the surrounding air overwhelmed her senses. It was too hot to see; too hot to breathe. The wooden framing crackled behind her. Electricity popped and arced. Then, an explosion.

The HVAC unit's container of Puron soared past its pressure capacity from the heat. Ava was launched like a bullet away from the burning building, away from the on-looking Greys, and away from the Lord of Violence—Nathan the Cursed.

-6-
HOUNDS OF HELL

Ava jerked her head up from the hard Earth. Her ears buzzed like a bag of angry hornets. Dry leaves and blades of grass dangled from her loc'd mohawk. Half of her face was peppered with loose pieces of soil. The shoulder and hip that she landed on ached.

Ava saw a hint of movement. Through the dark smoke that lingered near the destroyed dry goods store, Nathan appeared like the fabled ninja. Two of the store's walls had crumbled from the explosion, exposing its innards. Though the store and most of the buildings in the area were advertised as accurate recreations of the town's original buildings, the backroom that was now exposed to the Montanan night sky was filled with nothing but present-day amenities. Ava scurried backward away from Nathan's advance. Her hands and feet worked in tandem to keep her butt off the ground.

The tide had turned; that is if it had ever been on her side in the first place. Ava was not prepared. She knew that now. Her ace in the hole was nothing to the vast amount of power he had. She started her plan too soon. If only she had waited another month or two, or even a year. Ava could have been better equipped for a moment such as this. She could have acquired new spells and skills. Maybe she could have learned of some new secret to defeat such a monster. It was all too soon. Her heart raced a mile a minute, pumping like a sports car's pistons.

"Use me," a voice boomed in her head. "I can do it."

In an instant, Ava's muscles tightened from the declaration. Her lips pulled back to a sneer, exposing her bare clenched teeth. Air hissed from her mouth like a raging steam engine. *Not now.* Ava shouted internally. Her muscles eased, reverting to their normal plasticity. If her plan was ultimately lost, except for the slim possibility of escape, using it at this very moment would be a tremendous waste for both of them.

Nathan picked up his pace and widened his stride. Ava climbed to her feet and darted down the hill through the knee-high sagebrush towards the valley below and the tree line in the distance. She used gravity to assist her as she plowed down the hill. Ava high-stepped to avoid getting her feet tangled up in the tiny branches. The grass and brush trembled from her disturbance. Small animals scattered while squeaking as she approached. The vegetation clawed at her shoes and pants. She continued to run as fast as she could, swatting at the one or two insects that flew too close to her face.

Ava hit the bottom of the hill, heavy-footed. The abrupt change in the ground's angle challenged her balance but she managed to keep her pace. Her arms and legs pumped in quick succession. She could see the factory off to her left in the distance with two bulky metal containers rusting away near its loading dock.

Two or three more miles to go.

Her lungs burned like a furnace from the exertion. As Ava ran, her heart pumped madly. Her legs were like a feverish hamster's as it tried to outrun its exercise wheel. She could hear her heart pumping in her ears like a wild bass drum but nothing else. The night seemed as silent as a Buster Keaton film.

Ava could not go directly to the factory with Nathan and the Greys still in tow. Her best bet was to lose them in the darkness that made its home in between the thick of the trees. As she grew closer, the thin patchy grass turned lush, wild, and tall, occasionally tripping her up when her steps were too low.

The fireflies that spotted the valley danced in the air or climbed over the grass and brush. The nearby bugs scattered up from the ground, lighting the surrounding area like the stars that twinkled across the night sky. Ava slowed as the abundance of the fireflies became more apparent. There were, what looked like to be, thousands of them flashing around her.

Throughout all of her years with the Abyss, Ava had traveled across the country countless times, and throughout those years she had seen fireflies plenty of times but never like this, and not in Montana. The fireflies flashed rhythmically like a disco's strobe lights. A part of her mind wandered as she watched them. It tried to figure out a pattern in the flashing or some kind of image or object created through their collective glow.

Ava stopped a few feet before the edge of the forest. Its canopy made the thicket of the forest much darker than the surrounding area. A few of the glowing insects pulsed as they drifted past and breached the dividing line. In the darkness beyond, Ava noticed more of those yellow lights. They flashed, on and off, like a firefly's rump, but those lights were at least four times the size and moving in close-knit pairs. Each set of yellow lights seemed to be tethered to each other, never straying, in any direction.

What started as ten or twelve pairs grew into at least two dozen bouncing lights. Ava hesitated at the edge, deciding not to take a step past the border of the clearing to cross into the dark forest. Safety could always be found in the light where she could see things much clearer. Ava looked back to check on her pursuers' distance. She had been running as fast as she could down the slope and through the field that followed, but this delay could have ruined her significant lead. To Ava's surprise, Nathan and all the Greys that made up his posse never left the top of the hill.

Why did he stop? Ava looked back and forth from the tree line to the hilltop, unable to make up her mind. The dozens of yellow lights drew closer to the forest's edge. Their movements became more erratic as they moved closer. Ava looked back at the field she had previously run through. The thousands of fireflies continued to light up their tiny rumps randomly, but they seemed to have sped up. Some of those tiny insects drifted from one blade of grass to another and flashed at different intervals. She looked back at the dense, dark forest. The pairing of lights was now only several feet away and appeared to be slowing down or stopping.

After a few more moments, Ava's eyes finally were able to adjust to the low light. She began to see the hint of some silhouettes. Those floating spheres that initially looked like bloated fireflies that kept their lights burning longer than the others now looked more like large eyes. Those solid yellow eyes blinked as they stared in her direction. The more eyes that showed up, the more she noticed the sound of heavy breathing. Everything else that once was stirring in the brush or within the forest itself, fell absolutely silent. The surrounding was no longer drowned out by her thumping heart. There was true silence. Even the crisp mountain breeze that ruffled her hair held its tongue.

Sticks and dry leaves cracked and crunched under the mighty beast's weight, breaking the uneasy silence that loomed over the night. Trees moaned as the large figure passed between them. It panted like a wild dog. Plumes of steam expelled from its direction broke the tree line. Its exhaust drifted up through the cool air and dispersed into the night sky. One foot came out into the moonlight, slamming down into the soft soil. Its menacing paw sank ever so slightly into the dirt and grass. Its long, hairless, partially skinless snout and massive jaws followed.

Globs of saliva dripped from its pointy fangs. Its gums were as dark as congealed blood. Its yellow eyes, which sat close together and locked in Ava's direction, glowed like a kerosene lamp. The other owners of those numerous pairs of bright yellow eyes followed their leader and crept out of the shadows, one at a time. Their breath was rank. It wafted through the night air. They smelled of putrefied matter. They snickered together like a pack of stalking hyenas.

The pack collectively lifted their snouts and inhaled the air. Ava checked over her shoulder once again. The group of Greys stood still at the top of the hill surrounding Nathan like a crew of well-trained bodyguards. Their scents were probably like how Ava's is now, unfamiliar. They were all as safe as a wondering peep of chickens pecking away aimlessly in a wolf's den.

Hell Hounds, which are considered by most in the Abyss as the ultimate hunters, find their prey by following the stench of their sins that cling to them like a shadow, always trailing behind. Everyone in the world at the very least has been lightly seasoned in sin. Ava, on the other hand, had kept her roots in the Abyss for years. Because of that, like every other Traveler or Initiate, Ava's whole essence was soaked in it.

If Only For One Night

The Traveler's star, like the pendant that dangled from Rhea Kane's neck and was seared on the inside of Ava's left wrist, granted its owner safety from indiscriminate demons like the Black Locusts, Capatus Furem, and the dreaded Hell Hounds. But Kismet was right about the rules, well, most of them. They did not apply to Ava anymore. Her branding was almost worthless. Its inherent protection from the demons of the Abyss had all but worn off months ago.

Ava looked up and scanned the heavens. The sky was pitch black except for the twinkle of the outstretched cosmos that encapsulated the rising moon. Time was still ticking along, but for Ava, it was not moving fast enough.

The leading Hell Hound stepped out fully into the pale moonlight. It sniffed the ground as it walked. The grass twitched. Ava cautiously stepped back from the advancing Hell Hound, one step at a time. She moved as calmly as possible, taking her time to fill up her lungs and exhale to help with controlling her emotions.

The cool breeze was still blowing from the top of the hill down into the valley. Ava gambled on one of the Greys becoming too terrified to stay still. They would think about their past and the acts they had committed up to this point and then wonder, "Can it smell me?" or "Does it smell me?" Two simple questions that would easily lead them down the path where their more damning thoughts reside. Putting your life into question while a Hell Hound was anywhere nearby was a definite step in the wrong direction. After that quick moment of reflection, the Grey would become terrified for their life and take off running. That would inevitably cause a cascading effect amongst the rest of the group. With just one panicked Grey, you could cause a stampede. She smiled a devious smile that went unseen from the shadow that cloaked her face.

Just a few more minutes. All the fear she might have had drifted away and was replaced by the thoughts of the Grey's ranks being ripped apart by their own Hell Hounds once those beasts smelled the abundance of sin wafting from the Grey's pores. *Sweet poetic justice.*

Time continued to pass, but her perceived inevitable future did not come to be. Every single one of those shifty, new-blooded, Greys stood their ground like hardened Travelers or competent Initiates. The pack of Hell Hounds crept closer. Each one of them continued to sniff at the field of grass in the valley near Ava.

What happened? The average run-of-the-mill Grey was only two baby steps shy from being brand spanking new to the Abyss and to everything it may hold. Seeing a set of Hounds in real life for the first time, even at their considerable distance, should have frightened at least one or two of them to death no matter how hardened they believed they were. But none of them, not a single one, broke rank. Ava's heart raced, which was the exact opposite of how she needed to be at that moment.

Her rapid heart rate squeezed adrenaline throughout her body, which led to a burst of rambling, uncontrolled thoughts, and a sharp temperature rise. The night was too cold to have beads of sweat gather on her forehead into a glinting line of water, sodium, and oils, but that did not stop a similar effect from happening under her clothing. Sweat collected at her armpits. Ava's body betrayed her mind at a moment when both should have been on the same accord.

She did not feel the sweat that trickled down her back or smell the pheromones that radiated off her body. The new scent drifted through the air and took hold of the Hell Hounds. Their large nostrils pointed skyward, sucking in all the secrets her body whispered to the breeze.

The beasts picked up the scent in an instant and encircled her in the field. Their flat tongues slipped in and out of the front of their jaws as they growled and snarled, tasting the air.

Ava looked back at Nathan the Cursed one last time. He smiled and seemingly waved. It was an eerie sight, to say the least. For someone of his caliber and ranking, a smile would be the last thing you would want to see. In less than a minute, the few grizzled Greys that stood frozen around him, slowly and sporadically, faded into nothingness.

Erik McGowan

-7-
PRIDE

Pride—it sneaks up on you. It catches you by surprise. It lingers in the background while you focus on everything else around you. Then it slips in like water through the tiniest of cracks, slowly causing havoc to your foundation, destroying you from within while you dress up your outward appearance. Pride never strikes alone. It tailgates behind other disastrous behaviors. Then it takes full advantage of the distractions that those actions might have caused.

Over time it grows like jungle vines. It takes hold with thick roots, entrenching itself deep within. It burrows so deep that it becomes one with you, helping you make decisions, and keeping you safe from outsiders and naysayers. It protects you so completely that once those roots are finally unearthed, your subconscious, that part of you that should have noticed pride long ago and seen it as a threat, springs into action to protect it. You become willing to fight against yourself, tooth and nail, to defend your newly discovered friend.

Years of devotion and deliberate actions are needed to pull yourself free from its grip. It can take decades of constant pruning and patching holes to avoid falling back into its trap. Before Ava had come up with her grand plan to save her sweet brother, Ava thought she had put in the needed amount of time to rid herself of that vice. To Ava's dismay, some of those roots were still entrenched, and waiting in the depths of her psyche to bloom once again so they could ensnare her.

Pride had shown its tentacles a few times already that night. A couple of times it poked out while Ava dealt with the Greys inside the tavern. Its roots grew a bit larger when she gained what she thought was an upper hand against Nathan, at the top of the hill. But now, at this very moment, she had finally noticed its vines resurfacing.

Nathan might have set the trap after noticing her pride during their short fight or maybe she caused this herself and all he had to do was take advantage of the situation. It was a conundrum, much like the chicken or the egg question, but the answer did not lean toward a solution for the current situation with the Hell Hounds.

The Hell Hounds grew more aggressive as time ticked away. The pack's alpha scraped at the grass and soil with its huge front paws, kicking up chunks of dirt and plant matter. The rest of the Hell Hounds reacted in a similar fashion. They growled and bounded around, hopping from side to side. If it were not for their yellow eyes, and hideous patchwork skin, the hounds could have been confused for a pack of excited dogs ready for a game of fetch.

A few snapped in her direction. Their jaws clapped shut like bear traps. Through all their excitement, the Hell Hounds managed to stay in a relative formation. They dared not move on the prey before the leader had its chance. The alpha Hell Hound pushed its way through the circle and attacked with a speed that made a diving falcon look like a drifting leaf. Ava dove to the side as soon as she saw its body jerk forward. She avoided the main strike by a foot. Its broad tail, half the size of its body in length and thick as a phone pole, bashed into her as she tried to stand. She grunted from the force of the whipping tail. Ava was knocked two feet away into the tall grass.

Two of the runts from the pack snapped at her arms and legs while she was on her back. Ava knocked the Hell Hounds away with a couple of swift kicks to their snouts. The two yelped from the strikes and then darted back to the edge of the monstrous circle. Ava hopped back to her feet.

Ava stole a quick glance back at Nathan. He stood at the top of the hill, still as stone. He would know not to leave his spot until the hounds were able to finish their job. He was the Lord of Violence, but outside of his realm, his rank did not matter to demons such as the Hell Hounds. He needed the protection of the Traveler's Star like everyone else. Either Ava's soul and the others that she stole would be collected that night or his soul and essence would take their place. Their nose did not discriminate when it came to soiled souls.

The moon climbed closer to its apex. The worst time of the night was quickly approaching, and she had yet to make it to the safety of the abandoned factory. Her battle with the dozens of Hell Hounds continued for several more minutes. The Hell Hounds snapped and scratched at her flesh with their jagged teeth and large paws.

During a brief scuffle, Ava cracked the jaw of a smaller Hell Hound with a rock about the size of an average brick that she had hidden behind her back. Its eyes widened in shock from the strike. It yelped from the injury and sulked back to the edge of the forest. Its paws scratched at its face as it groaned. After it removed a few of its dislodged teeth, the Hell Hound rushed back to the battlefield.

Heat rose from Ava's body, dispersing into the air. Her heart pushed gallons of adrenaline throughout her body. Each vein and artery pulsated with hard thumps, forcing their way to the surface of her skin. Her brown eyes dilated, and the world grew sharp. She could hear her heart again, thumping through low growls that drifted from her lips. *Not yet. Not yet.*

Another voice, deeper than her own spoke, dominating her thoughts. "If not now—when," it demanded. The shock from its defiance caused a critical lapse in her guard.

Even without that inside information, the massive Hell Hounds managed to take full advantage of her lack of focus. One of the pack broke the ring that encircled her and rushed in. Its head and shoulders slammed into the back of Ava's legs, knocking her to the ground. She flopped face-first from the impact. The large alpha made its approach with two quick leaps. Its muzzle opened wide enough to fit half of her head inside. Its jagged teeth sank into her leg, cutting through her denim and flesh like a pair of scissors through papier mache.

Ava held in the pain. Nothing makes a beast wilder than an injured and moaning prey. She propped herself up and punched the Hell Hound's hairless snout with all her might. Her off-balanced punch did not affect the Hell Hound in the slightest. The Hound growled ferociously before crunching down on her leg, cracking her fibula in several places. Ava reached for her shattered leg. She could feel its broad tongue vibrating from its snarl. Then it shook her. The great beast shook Ava like a rag doll or a chew toy or an expensive slipper in the jaws of an excited pup.

She tried her best to hold on and wrench its jaws open, but the whipping force was too much. Her body flailed around, smacking against the soft dirt, bouncing from the impact. The fireflies that were flying by or crawling around scattered from the disturbance. Their yellow, fluorescent abdomens stayed dark for the first time that night. The rest of the Hell Hounds jumped back to avoid Ava's limp body.

After the first couple of whips, Ava tucked her head between her arms for protection. Nothing was working. She could not hold on and she could not stop the concussive force. She was dazed and confused. The world around her began to swim. Her arms collided with the ground and then with the sides of her face. That same angry voice from before cried out again, "When?"

"Not yet. I can't use you like this," she whispered, trying her best to stay conscious. Ava felt the mixture of saliva and blood dripping down her leg. Even though the soil was soft compared to the graveled parking lot behind the tavern, her head and shoulders ached all the same from the impacts.

After a couple more violent shakes, the Hell Hound released her leg. Blood dripped from its mouth, thick and viscous. Ava rolled over to her stomach. She was done with trying to hide from her present condition. She was hurt, bad. Ava moaned like an injured deer. Attempting to escape, Ava dragged her body, inch by inch, with her elbows. Every movement was agony. She was barely able to see where she was going. The grass around her was not that tall but it was thick and full.

Ava did not care where she ended up. Anywhere was probably better than where she was right now. And escaping, like when she faced the full fury of Nathan the Cursed, was the only solution she could think of.

"Get you some sort of distance between you and those Hell Hounds, and then come up with another plan," a voice said.

The voice was right. Ava could not stay around here and strategize with the threat of another attack looming over her head. Her leg was shot, and her enemies probably stood around her at every angle. She could only guess. Ava could hear them, prowling, growling, barking. But the pain... she could not focus through all the pain. Maybe there was a gap in their formation somewhere. She could slip through unnoticed like a gentle breeze. Maybe they somehow lost her scent in the grass and the toiled soil. Ava could only hope.

As Ava dragged herself through the brush and grass, the Hell Hounds, even the mighty alpha, abruptly sat where they stood and then laid down. Ava stopped in her tracks when she heard them go quiet. She looked around at them, barely seeing the tops of their heads through the grass that stood in the forefront of her vision. They remained still in the grass, obedient as show dogs. Then she heard a faint sound. The sound of crinkling grass as something, most likely someone, approached. "Nathan," she whispered, gritting her teeth.

"I'm only going to ask once," Nathan said. He stopped beside her head.

Ava looked over at his clunky boots, barely lifting her head off the ground. Nathan shoved her body over with a kick. His size eleven boot crashed into her face, just above her eye. She reflexively grabbed the area, while rolling over to her back. She felt the blood rush to her brow as it swelled from the impact. With her free eye, Ava looked up at him. His smile was as jagged as a twisted hand saw. Ava looked back down at his feet. They were steel-toed boots. She did not notice that earlier. That explained the incredible pain. Her head thumped like a pair of shoes in the dryer.

"You look like you have something to say," he said.

Ava coughed, a deep throaty cough several times. Her throat was drying out from his proximity. She moved her hand to show him what he did to her face. Her eye squinted. It was bloodshot and watery. The knot right above her eyebrow had grown to the size of a ping-pong ball in a few seconds. "Hurry up," she shouted. She clenched her teeth to bear the pain that she knew was soon to come, and it did.

He stomped on her chest. Ava rocked from the pain, wrapping her arms around her body. She did not cry out or even whimper. She held every bit of the pain in, only letting some of it show through the grimace on her face. Nathan dropped down onto her stomach, his legs straddling her waist. His two-hundred-pound-plus frame expelled the air she had bottled up in her lungs. Next, came the punch to her ribs. She howled. Her body contorted from the agony.

Nathan waited for Ava to calm down and catch her breath. He punched her again in the ribs, on the same side. She thought she felt something snap. He was going to beat her to death. She knew it. In her mind, her death by his cursed hands was as certain as her name. Fear once again made its home in her heart.

This time, through the excruciating pain, Ava tried to buck him off. She twisted and thrust her hips like a wild bronco, but he rode her like a skilled cowboy. The next hit was across her face. His fist slammed into her cheek. Her face snapped to the opposite side. The inside of her mouth was split from her teeth. The blood from her mouth splashed on the nearby grass. The smell of fresh blood and the introduction of more violence caused the Hell Hounds to stir and whine.

The noises that came from the excited pack of Hounds sounded muffled and distant to Ava. She tried for a second time to get away. Ava pushed at his hips but barely moved his muscular torso. Her arms were still weak and feeble. They fumbled at his body, scraping at his neck and chest. He punched her again. The punch landed squarely at Ava's temple. Her arms fell limp to her sides. She moaned. Once again, in such a short span of time, Ava was struggling to stay conscious. Her legs squirmed under his weight.

"No, no, no." He smacked her across the face with the back of his hand and then seized her by the chin. "Wake up. I didn't ask my question yet."

She opened her eyes to thin slits. The defiance she once had was now beaten out of her.

"Gooood. Now," he said as he climbed off her. The bloodthirsty Hell Hounds stood up to their haunches, fidgeting and whining. Their jaws snapped as their tongues flicked in and out like a sniffing snake. "The question of the day… Where are the souls?"

She winced from the pain flowing to her brain from seemingly every inch of her body. Her teeth were stained from blood. "Impetus…," she said in a hushed tone. The words barely reached Nathan's ears over the anxious Hell Hounds.

"Speak. Louder." He kicked her wounded leg.

The pain surged through her calf to the rest of her body like a bolt of lightning. She shouted with every bit of energy and anger she could muster. "Impetus."

Nathan's brow tightened. It had been decades since Nathan the Cursed had been confused by the statement from one of his victims. The poor souls would either beg for forgiveness, cry for mercy, or sometimes, on rare occasions, do both. Other times they would stay steadfast for a few moments, not unlike what Ava tried to do moments ago, but they all would turn into blubbering sacks of meat after he started to lay it in on them. They would usually start their vain attempts to sway his position in their native tongue and then slowly switch to incoherent cries for absolution. But Latin? The abruptness of the word, 'impetus,' was like a slap in the face. It surprised and shocked him. Nathan froze in place like a deer in headlights as his mind mulled over the word and its meaning.

Within seconds, Nathan was tackled by the alpha Hell Hound. He hit the ground face first, several feet away from Ava. The Hound pounced on his back, trying to lock its mighty jaws around his neck. He shouted for them to sit still but none of them listened. Each Hell Hound lunged at him in turn. He caught a few of them by the throat and launched them into the tree line. Their limp bodies battered against the stiff tree trunks. Nathan franticly patted around his neck and chest. His medallion was missing. He looked over at Ava.

Ava pushed herself up to a sitting position so she could see better. His eight-pointed star medallion, the mark of safe passage, was clutched in Ava's hand. Outside the realms of the Abyss, anyone without the protection of the Traveler's Star was fair game to the demons that might roam free on the Earth. And even though Nathan ruled the Ring of Violence and fought in a few of the wars that ravaged the Kingdom and the Abyss, his origins were the same as any other man.

Fear and despair, emotions that had faded from Nathan's consciousness for hundreds of years, now oozed from his pours, sending the pack of Hell Hounds into a frenzy. It mixed with his abundance of violent sins like a Louisiana gumbo. His pungent scent was stronger than anything Ava's body could ever muster.

Nathan fought back as best he could, ripping off limbs, impaling eyes, and snapping bones like toothpicks, but the Hell Hounds kept coming back. The wounds that Nathan inflicted on the Hell Hounds began to regenerate a minute or two after the injury. And in the end, his greatest ability, the deadly Hellfire, had absolutely no effect on them. As Ava watched Nathan the Cursed struggle with the Hell Hounds, she forced herself to a standing position, balancing most of her weight on her good leg. Her goal had not changed, but her destination changed back to its original location, the old factory.

A couple more miles to go. Ava limped away, one painful step at a time, toward the large factory and away from Nathan's screams. The sound scattered through the cool night's air. His bones cracked and his flesh was torn. Ava did not need to see what was going on between him and the Hell Hounds. In fact, Ava did not want to see. Revenge has never been the path to success. The field of victory will be covered with the bodies of those who tried to stop her plans. Justice will be her weapon, not revenge.

Besides, Ava knew what was going to happen. His soul and fate were sealed. The reward for failure is the same for everyone alike. One tortured soul will be taken by the Hell Hounds to the realm where all who climbed the Abyss will surely return to in the end.

Ava heard the unmistakable sound of a Gate to the Abyss crack open. The Hell Hounds dragged Nathan's tattered body following the alpha through the breech. The immediate threat was now gone. She stopped in place. The cool night's air blew over her heated skin, ruffled her hair, and tickled her nose with hints of sulfur. Ava wiped her face with the back of her hand. Blood streaked across her forearm.

The five-story factory loomed in the distance, slowly growing in size as Ava lumbered towards its brick hide. Ava used some of the trees to help stabilize her new awkward gait. Her ears were still ringing as if she had been standing next to a speaker set to its max level for hours. Her head ached as well. It was a dull pain; unlike the jolts she received every time her leg's wounds touched some foreign object or when her foot hit the ground too hard or when she forgot and let too much weight rest on her busted leg.

Ava wanted it to end. She wanted all of it to end. The night was long and seemingly never-ending. *A few more steps. That's it.* Ava chanted to herself. Every several feet, Ava stopped to look around for Greys roaming the valley or the possible other demons lurking in the shadows beneath the forest's canopy. She strained to hear over the squealing of tinnitus for anything that would try to sneak up from one of her many blind spots.

If Only For One Night

Through extreme pain and exertion, Ava made it to the factory.

***

Ava moaned as she lifted her T-shirt. A large reddish-purple blotch covered the left side of her rib cage. She inhaled, mentally preparing herself before gently touching the bruise. The pain was as intense as if her light touch was another powerful punch from Nathan the Cursed. Her hand retracted in a flash. Ava looked around just as fast, scanning the area to see if anything was nearby. There was still the possibility of straggling Greys or maybe some stalking demons creeping through the dark forest or crossing the nearby river.

Ava's ears perked up. She went stiff. Did she hear something or was that her imagination? Ava was not sure. In high-stress situations, the mind has a habit of making up scenarios to keep itself ready for any situation that may come. After a few moments, Ava relaxed.

Ava gingerly pulled off her shirt, wincing the whole way through. She dropped it to the side of the rusty roll-off dumpster. Its dirty teal paint was scratched, and it flaked near its metal wheels. The wooden boards underneath were warped and ragged from the weight. Ava looked around again. The thought of modesty popped into her head for a brief second. Her arms jumped, wanting to cover up her exposed skin and sports bra. Earlier that day, Ava had considered wrapping her breast with an ace bandage for more support and control throughout the night, but the convenience store in the nearby town didn't have what she needed. She had also heard about how, if bound too tight, could cause breathing problems, among other things. Within that split second, Ava immediately buried that thought with more pressing matters.

On her stomach were two black rings surrounding her belly button like the rings of a bull's eye. She lowered herself to the ground, leaning against the factory's brick wall for support as she descended. Ava laid down on the concrete behind the roll-off dumpster to help hide herself from any onlookers. Behind her head, Ava placed her rolled-up shirt. Her skin was now gooseflesh. She placed her thumbs and index fingers around the outermost rings on her stomach. With closed eyes, she concentrated, using a meditation technique suggested to her by her one-time therapist, Lara Zeiger.

After the incident, Ava's parents thought it would be a good idea for her to talk to someone. They tried to be that open ear several times, but Ava would not let them into what she was going through. So, they decided to get help from a professional. The weekly sessions lasted for a few months but there was a minimal amount of talking from Ava's side of the room. And once Ava reached legal age and could make her own decisions, she refused to go back. Within those months, Lara Zeiger tried her best to reach Ava. She wanted Ava to open up about the incident that occurred outside of the park.

Lara experimented with different techniques to elicit a response from Ava, but the bulk of her attempts never worked. The failure of those techniques, based on the consensus of her more senior advisors, could not have been from Ava's stubbornness as Lara originally thought, but from Lara's lack of experience and skills. Ava was, they were quick to point out, only the second patient she had ever seen in her professional career. But in the end, the one thing that stuck with Ava was the storm cloud meditation technique.

"It's easy," Mrs. Zeiger said. "You've already got the first part down." She smiled.

Ava was lying back on the couch, studying the office's drop ceiling, trying to find a pattern or two in its pitted surfaces.

Mrs. Zeiger cleared her throat. "Close your eyes." She waited for Ava to oblige her before continuing. "Picture yourself in a wide-open field. Any kind of field. Or maybe a beach if you like."

Ava had been stuck in the Midwest all her life. She was tired of seeing endless fields and snow-capped mountains. Picturing herself on the beach held way more appeal. Even though Ava had never been to an actual beach before, she had a general idea of what it would be like. She imagined a mixture of all the golden beaches she had seen on television shows and movie screens, with their clear blue skies as far as the eye could see. The imagined beach was full of people running around, swimming, children splashing about, women laying out on their large blankets sunbathing under their large umbrellas, with others playing volleyball or dancing to music blaring from small radios.

"What are you imagining?"

Ava did not respond. She was lost in her own world, enjoying the sights and sounds of the people and the crashing waves.

The fact that Ava did not answer was not a cause of concern for Ms. Zeiger. She continued to follow the script. "Keep picturing it. That is your life. That's all of the good times from your past, present, and future. Take it in. Smell the fresh air. Feel the breeze on your face and through your hair. Let the sun warm your skin."

Ava loved it there in her imagined land. It was almost everything she ever wanted. She wanted to spend the rest of their sessions in this sunny world. If only she could be there, right now. If she could somehow escape from her mundane life, here in this drab office with Mrs. Zeiger, and travel to some remote beach or island where she did not have to talk about her past. Some place where she could be born anew, where no one knows her, and she could live life any way she would like.

"Now imagine," Mrs. Zeiger continued, "in the distance, some storm clouds are looming at the edge of the horizon," Mrs. Zeiger said.

Ava's brow tightened as she imagined the darkening clouds collecting in the distance. The wind on the beach picked up, blowing down some of the umbrellas that leaned ever so slightly in the warm sand. Each set of waves grew larger by the minute. Their crests foamed like a rabid dog's mouth, sending the people who were wading a few feet into the surf back to their towels and other belongings. The sky shifted to a dark gray as the clouds covered the golden sun. Within a few minutes, which in the real tangible world was only a few seconds, all the beachgoers had cleared out the area except for Ava. She stood on that deserted beach, scared, cold, and alone.

"Those dark stormy clouds that are collecting in the sky, they are filled with everything bad that has ever happened or will happen to you or around you."

The sky cracked like a bullwhip. Torrential rain poured out from its opening. Ava shivered in the chilly rain, desperate for shelter, but there was none. She wanted to leave but could not. Ava could not escape her imaginary world. She was stuck there in the sand like the lifeguard chair a half-mile or so down the beach.

"Like those storm clouds and the rain that they carry with them, pain and suffering will, at times, drift in and ruin a perfectly good day. It happens to all of us, including myself. But you can get through it. Remember—it will not last forever, much like those storm clouds that are starting to thin. All that anger, fear, resentment, angst… let it all drift away with those clouds. Watch as they travel off into the distance, freeing up the sun once more."

The left side of Ava's face twitched a few times from the thought of Mrs. Lara Zeiger and her meditative instructions. The thoughts of pain, fear, anger, and frustration that had collected over the past few hours drifted from the forefront of her mind like those dark ominous clouds on a summer breeze. Ava let out a deep exhale as the clouds drifted off into the distance of her mind's eye.

"It's your turn," Ava said.

"Thank you," a timid voice echoed in her head. Gluttony was finally done and by the end of this night, it will be free.

"Re…dundantiam," Ava muttered.

The rings on her stomach spun, revolving in opposite directions. They started slow, then doubled in speed every couple of seconds. As they spun, the black rings thinned out.

Ava's world went black.

-8-
BLACK AS PITCH

5 months ago.

Golden Shark Ink was a failing tattoo parlor with an on-again off-again owner whose presence at the shop was a roll of the dice. The Golden Shark so far had been in business for ten years but recently the tattoo parlor has been struggling to keep its doors open. Its main entrance was in a small, dingy alley between E. 23rd Street and S. 15th Avenue. Because of the owner's sporadic attendance, walk-ins, their prime source of business, started to dry up; leaving them with nothing but word of mouth, which on most occasions, was almost entirely negative.

Throughout Ava's travels, she had stopped in several tattoo parlors throughout the country like the Dry Dock, Inked Up Tattoos, and the seedy Davey Jones Locker Ink in Chattanooga. Ava also tried a few international shops and backroom clubs throughout Europe and Southeast Asia. Each and every one of them rejected her business for one main reason. Ava wanted them to only use the ink that she would provide. Even though the mention of a customer's ink being used is not explicitly written about in OSHA compliance, the idea of that to the people in the business was quite taboo. But, unlike the others, the Golden Shark and its owner could not afford to say no to her requests. He was past due on everything and soon the collectors would come by to collect.

Ava had the cash and in the end, that was all that really mattered. The complexity of her request did not come in the form of the tattoos themselves, but rather the instructions she had for each set of tattoos.

The owner looked over his shoulders, checking the street for snooping bystanders or nosy vagrants who might hear bits and pieces of their transaction. They were not in the toughest neighborhood, by no stretch of the imagination, but he did have his debts.

"For each tattoo, I have specific ink I want you to use. The bottles will be labeled," Ava said.

His mouth opened slightly.

Her hand shot up in front of his face. "Please don't ask why."

His lips tightened.

"Most of the tattoos will be simple circles with words cut out."

"What are the words?" He asked with some reservations. He was not sure if that question went against her previous request.

"Here's the list." Ava handed him a sheet of lined paper. Its edges were frayed from being ripped out of a cheap composition book. She did not bother buying the book the sheet came from. Jotting down your plans can be a recipe for disaster. One unforeseen circumstance and Ava could lose the book somewhere. Next thing you know, all of her planning, strategies, and private thoughts would be out there for all to see like a slow-walking streaker. Instead, Ava ripped the last two pages out the back of the book while pretending to shop for school supplies at the local convenience store.

The words were written in print with large letters to avoid any confusion. The sheets also contained several of the designs. They were rough sketches, but each was detailed enough to be understood by a competent artist. "They need to be in that exact order," she said. "Do you understand?"

He scanned over the papers. "Yes." He responded correctly. It was exactly what Ava expected to hear but he did not sound as confident as she would have liked.

"In that exact order. No artistic or creative expression. I need it to be exact." She stared at him, unblinking.

He nodded, only briefly holding eye contact. "I got it. No changes."

"I'll pay half now and half after you've finished. How does that sound?" Ava pulled out a wad of cash from her black duffle bag. She handed it to him without counting.

She could see it on his face and through the way he held the cash between both his hands. She could see it in his eyes. The gears in his mind turned, trying to figure out what he would spend his newfound wealth on first.

Greed.

If the offer is high enough, people are willing to do anything and everything with no questions asked. They could be wandering around with arms full, covered in riches and extravagance, but they will still scrounge for more. Blinded by their greed, they are unable to see that they might already have enough. Greed is what put the owner of the Golden Shark into this position in the first place. The 'need for more' had been constantly pulling at his heart and mind for years. His willingness to give up what he might have for more of what he probably did not need was his constant weight to bear. It was an anchor that slowly dragged him down, until his face was barely above the waterline—head tilted, gasping for air through puckered lips.

"Sure." He stared at the money in his hands. His eyes were wide like a set of curtains drawn completely open as he scanned over the assortment of bills. He did not bother to count it. From what he saw, the majority of it was hundred-dollar bills. That handful alone was more money than he had ever held in his hands throughout his colorful life. He looked around again, checking for peepers or eavesdroppers. It was a grimy alley that they were conducting business near after all. "This isn't going to come back to haunt me, is it?" He looked back down at the money. Some of the bills fell from his hands onto the sidewalk. "You know what, I didn't just ask that." He looked at Ava's handwritten note again. "I'm your man."

She smiled and brushed a few of her locs to the side. "Good."

"Be seeing you," he said.

***

Ava arrived the following night after mentally preparing herself for the long haul. Over the last few years, Ava did not like to sit still for too long in an area she was unfamiliar with. She had to keep moving. Staying one step ahead was good but several steps was always better.

The decrepit look of the alley and the shop's entrance did not do the inside justice. It was by no means immaculate but the assumption that everything inside would be worn down, old, or covered with duct tape was gratefully not the case. The Golden Shark was, for the most part, just like any other inner-city tattoo shop. The main hallway contained pictures of previous customers smiling like they just won the lottery while they showed off their new tattoos. One of those customers was a famous comedian. There were some band members from Brutal, a Finnish Death Metal cover band, and Taking Tuesdays Off, a new pop-rock band that had a couple of number-one singles. There was also a picture of a radio host from Power Play radio, WKPP, and a couple of other local celebrities that Ava could not place. On the walls, between each station were hand-drawn tattoo samples from each of the artists to showcase their skill level and what original art was still for sale.

The hired help, two young and hip tattoo artists, Chris and Bam, brought in most of the new clientele for the past five years. Most of the band members and their roadies were tattooed by those two. When the owner brought the idea to them earlier that evening, they protested about the new job assignment as much as the owner did the previous day. Even though new work had mainly trickled in for the last nine months, the duo had other clientele and previous commitments that they needed to take care of first.

"It takes at the very least two weeks to heal from each full session. With that amount of skin… you should do this over a couple of months," they each told the owner in their own way. Chris and Bam were collectively preaching to the choir. He already knew all of that, but he would not budge. So, the two tattoo artists decided to tell Ava the same thing, hoping she would change her mind and soften her rushed scheduling.

Their opinions and expertise on the subject did not matter to Ava in the slightest either. This was something that needed to be done. There would be no turning back or delay. The catalyst for this journey had already happened and Ava could not fight the current that dragged her along. No amount of backpedaling will stop the flow of time or reverse it.

Ava's plan did not need the two of them, but with three instead of one, the entire process could go by much quicker. With a few more big-faced bills added to the pot, Chris and Bam switched their opinion just as quickly as the owner. They ditched all of their appointments as fast as they grabbed up the cash. *Everything in this world has a price, including the people that inhabit it.* Ava knew that better than most.

The trio got to work, following Ava's instructions like some sacred text. Each session was set up so that the tattoo artists would complete a full section at a time. Even though each tattoo would be created with just black ink, the process took much longer than they had expected.

For several hours a night, Ava would lie still on the cushioned table. Her mind would either wander, helping her to tune out the buzzing from the tattoo machines and the sting of the needles, or she would sleep like a napping cat. Sometimes Ava muttered to herself. Her whispers, at times, gained the attention of Chris and Bam, but not the experienced owner of the Golden Shark. They would lean in while her eyes were closed to try and hear better or attempt to read her moving lips. Their attempts were as futile as reading the lips of a babbling newborn.

When the tattoo design called for a mirror image on the opposite side of Ava's body, two of the tattoo artists would work in tandem. Black bands were placed around her arms, starting halfway up her forearms, and stopping right below the start of her shoulders. There were four bands in total for each arm, spaced out evenly with the words, ira, rixa, and furia, through their middles. Her legs matched with the same opaque bands but with the words, ignavus and segnis. The letters looked to be etched out of the ink to show her brown skin beneath.

Her stomach received two thick circles. The smallest one was placed around her belly button. The largest stopped just below her solar plexus. The words, poena and porcus, were etched out of both circles. All three of the tattoo artists admired her chiseled six-pack with raised eyebrows and hushed tones. Ava slept through most of that session. Her dark brown eyes danced under their lids.

Her palms had two different and distinct symbols. On her left, a silhouette of a small dog, something akin to a Beagle, was crafted with jagged lines like a wall that was made by stacking various kinds of stones. The one etched into her right palm was in the shape of a poison dart frog. Its bulging eyes and spots were represented using negative space. The team of tattooists had their most 'fun' on the animals. Those tattoos were not as mundane as the rest. Ava's only instructions on the matter were the type of animals to be used, which ink container for each, and to keep the design simple. Ava did not want to end up with museum art on her palms to appease their stylistic fetishes.

On the last day, the trio worked on Ava's back. The back of her shoulders was adorned with one circle each. And like the other tattooed bands and rings, each one had a word etched out of them; cupiditas, and concupisco.

During most of the process, the two junior tattoo artists muttered amongst themselves about the purpose of the words and symbols. They came up with wildly imaginative stories about the possible reasons. The two, Chris and Bam, never asked Ava a single question to see if their ideas matched up with reality in any form. There was no point in missing out on a large payout from being too nosy about something that, after their last session, probably will never affect them at all. But knowing that they could mistakenly breach the contract and lose out on a good score did not stop their inquiring minds. The two would, at times, spend hours before or after a session coming up with different scenarios on why she wanted the tattoos and why all of it had to be such a secret.

The owner did not participate in any of their backroom conversations about their secretive client. Ever since the first day, they discussed Ava's rush to have the job finished, his only input into the conversation was twofold, "Don't ask her any questions. Not even to offer her a drink of water or to see if she needs a break," and, "curiosity killed the cat, and I don't have eight lives to spare." He still had as many questions as he did the first day he met her, but those questions would stay private like the secrets of a forgotten journal. No one needed to know his thoughts on the matter, let alone himself. "Finish the job, get your money, and move the hell on." The rest of the crew might not listen, but he made it his motto and mantra. He would repeat that phrase to himself anytime a question would arise.

After their final tattoo session and receiving the remaining half of their bounty, the reluctant trio parted ways for good. A few weeks later, the Golden Shark was shut down. The shop was left boarded up and abandoned like the rest of the buildings on that failing block of downtown real estate. Its owner skipped town, spending the shop's late rent money on a plane ticket and a down payment on permanent lodging in Ireland where he would live out his days on its coasts, escaping the debts he had accrued over a couple of decades in the States. His move was bittersweet but much needed. The United States was his home, but it was time to make a fresh start.

The other two, Chris and Bam, scattered to the wind. They made their new homes at different parlors, as far away from the Golden Shark as they could get without leaving the country. Each one of the tattooing trio kept their word until the end. They never spoke of that private four-night session for that peculiar woman amongst themselves or to anyone else. Their lips stayed sealed., even though from time to time, their minds did wonder.

-9-
BRICKS AND MORTAR

Ava took a deep breath as her consciousness made its way back to the foreground. Still groggy, she opened her eyes, blinking several times to gain her faculties. Above her was an inevitable sight, the pale moon. Round and full, it hung in the sky at its apex. Her heart trembled. Adrenaline flooded her cells. Panic crept through her mind. How long had she been asleep? How long had the moon been at its peak? She could not tell one way or the other. Ava had lost precious time, but she had also fully recovered thanks to Gluttony. Her wounds were healed, and her fatigue was long gone.

The skin around her ribs had reverted to its normal brown shade. The knot on her forehead had shrunk and the skin smoothed. The cuts in her mouth from her teeth were sealed shut. The pain in her sternum which added to her shallow breathing was now gone. The blood that seeped from her gnawed leg had long since stopped and the holes were filled in like nothing ever happened. All of Ava's injuries and accumulated exhaustion from the past several hours had disappeared, leaving her as capable as she was before the night had begun.

Ava bounced to her feet. She dusted off her clothes, starting from the bottom of her pants. Ava picked up her shirt and shook it before putting it back on.

***

Ava's haven, the old Eastern Snowberry Co. factory, was once a prominent job site for this once-booming town. The building started as a small housing complex, situated close to the river where the town's name arrived, for the miners in the area. The company that owned the mine, Eastern Snowberry Co., decided that it would be in their best interest to give its workers free housing as an incentive for the back-breaking, fourteen-hour, six days a week, workdays. Their housing was by no means spectacular, but it was a welcomed change of pace for the average miner's living conditions in the region. They would get three square meals a day and a warm place to stay, and that was all right with them.

With all the wealth that was being generated and the mine's ample amount of work, the town, which was mainly just a few dozen miners, two foremen, and a small trading post for basic goods, doubled and then tripled in size within its first decades. People from all over the country came to the booming town for a stable job at the Eastern Snowberry mine or to set up a business to capitalize off their worker's fortunes. A few of the prominent papers in the region like the Midwest Regional called North Forks, "…the new Butte, Montana. 'The second richest hill on Earth'".

Everyone wanted to be a part of that exciting new town. As the money came pouring in, the miners were able to afford their own housing. Eastern Snowberry Co.'s housing complex that had been used for the workers was renovated and converted into a state-of-the-art foundry that produced cast iron stoves and other metallurgic molds. The molds were created by using crushed sand created from the excavated rocks that came from the mine. Eastern Snowberry Co.'s profits soared from all of its new business endeavors.

Over the next four decades, North Forks continued to boom, causing several other towns to spring up like Bitterroots on its outskirts. Klink bloomed fifteen miles to the south, near the Black Wash cliffs. The town of Bearing broke ground in the dense forests to the east, between two of the forks of the river. The town of Red Glen, which was the closest, was founded three and a half miles northeast of the town's center by a crew of loggers who supplied the fresh lumber that was fundamental to the expansion of each of the settlements.

All of that changed in the late 19th century. The value and abundance of the mined material, silver, had been on the decline for years. Seeking more product and profit, several of the Eastern Snowberry Co.'s board members ordered their foremen to speed up the excavation and dig deeper tunnels throughout the mountain. The majority of the miners followed without a single question. They figured that more profits for the company meant higher wages for them. So, they burrowed through the mountainous earth like giant earthworms. Without guidance from regulations or careful planning, plus the lack of experience of the younger, more spirited miners, several of the newly formed tunnels collapsed, instantly killing or trapping over one hundred hardworking, blue-collared men underground. With their conventional methods, there was no conceivable way to reach the trapped workers in time to save their lives. So, any rescue attempt that was suggested was deemed worthless. The 'Second richest hill in America' and the town of North Forks, which fed off its mountainous innards, was now forever marred by preventable deaths.

Three months before the incident, one of the board members for the Eastern Snowberry Co., Gary Hicks 3rd, convinced the majority of board members to open life insurance policies for each new and senior employee that joined their business as either a factory worker or miner. With all of the employees on their insurance, the Eastern Snowberry Co. could keep two dollars a week from each employee's pay. None of them would have ever guessed that their scheme to siphon off money from their employees would ultimately backfire.

Over a period of eighteen months, the surviving family members of the victims who died or were trapped in the tunnel collapse incident received their payouts from the employee's mandatory life insurance policy. With their newfound wealth, many of the recipients decided to leave North Forks in a great exodus that was only rivaled by Moses and the Israelites. They scattered across Montana to bigger, more well-established cities like Billings and Great Falls or they left the state of Montana altogether for other parts of the country. Some trekked to the major cities on the east and west coasts. Others, not quite willing to give up rural life, spent most of their riches buying plots of land in different states throughout the plains of the Midwest.

The once vibrant town was now on its last leg. It hemorrhaged its citizens like blood from an open wound. Its immense potential dried up like its abandoned silver mine. The surrounding towns that blossomed from North Forks' scraps, did not fare well either. Each one of the satellite towns came extremely close to sharing the same fate as their bigger brother. Their populations shrank as Eastern Snowberry Co. struggled to make ends meet with their cast iron stove business and their massive shortage of reliable employees. Even though cast iron products were still in high demand, the profits were not enough to pay for the high wages, taxes, and other business expenses while keeping the company afloat amongst the life insurance payouts. With sustainable small-town jobs and trade, the bordering towns managed to outlive their once-bright star. North Forks, the miner's town, was completely abandoned in August of 1934.

By the mid-1980's a new trend began to sweep through the rural mid-west. Children from those small sleepy towns who were lured away by the bright lights and big city life that they saw on their color televisions, began to travel out-of-state for college or uprooted themselves to start their adulthood in those exciting cities. They left their families behind but took with them their sense of community, manners, and most importantly, their stories of small-town life.

Some of those fast-paced 'city folk' grew intrigued by those stories. They too were searching for something different. They wanted to get closer to nature by escaping the big cities, transporting themselves to a simpler time when everyone was not in such a rush. They wanted to sit on their porch, rocking in a big wooden chair, drinking a glass of cold lemonade, while watching the sunset. They wanted to grow their own food and raise their own livestock.

People began to make pilgrimages to those small towns, by the dozens at first, to see what it was really like firsthand. Soon, tourism in those areas exploded and became the new cash cow for local businesses. Red Glen was one such town. Old, dilapidated buildings that were slated to be demolished were now being restored to their former glory.

Day trips and historic tours to the old mining town, North Forks, were created and sold out within hours of their tickets being up for sale. Throughout late spring to early fall, Red Glen's population would swell by a thousand, from all of the visitors. It was like a modern-day gold rush. Most of Red Glen's citizens did not care for the influx of out-of-towners while they were there, but they did enjoy the financial benefits of their annual migrations. Over time, North Forks became an extension of Red Glen. The factory, the last standing building from the old mining town, was cleaned up and turned into a museum with a gift shop and restaurant installed on the fourth floor.

But, once again, the tides had started to turn. With the popularity of personal computers in the late 90s, the explosion of the Internet in the early 2000s, and the invention of digital photography, the need to actually be physically in an area became less of a necessity for the newer generations. Tourism to the area slowed down immensely. The finishing touch came with the incident of 2007. It took the once booming tourism, which by this point was already on a downswing, soaked it in gasoline, and lit its corpse on fire.

Once tourism stopped, all the major construction in the area screeched to an abrupt halt. The construction company did not bother taking most of their supplies with them. They left everything where it was and chalked it up as a loss for tax purposes. Red Glen's citizens were deflated. "Clean and pristine" was the town's motto for a decade or two, but the newer, and younger politicians who took over after the collapse, would say, "Why clean up a so-called mess when you don't have any guests?" A slogan that would have probably sat extremely well with your average adolescent.

The Eastern Snowberry Co. factory, most of the antique buildings that were refurbished, and the dozen or so reconstructed buildings for the tourists fell into shambles. They were unkempt and ultimately unwanted by most of the local residents.

Ava was different. She saw what that factory had been, and she could also see what it could be. The Eastern Snowberry Co. factory was an anchor to the past and a place of safety throughout the night. It would be easy to protect and navigate while giving her plenty of places to hide out if the night called for it.

The silver moon was high in the sky. Its pale face peaked through the cracked and broken skylights like a peeping tom in the night. The inside of the dilapidated factory was as cold as the outside. Ava stepped in carefully. She passed through the dim guest entrance next to a dusty, paint-chipped ticket booth. Its plexiglass was cloudy with hints of a pale yellow across its face. Two rolls of dusty tickets leaned against its window. Ava stepped past the booth and made her way towards the factory floor.

Ava crept through a set of double doors, opening one side just enough to slip through. Her steps were quick but as silent as a skipping astronaut on the moon. She stopped for a moment and pressed up against the wall on the far end of the building, engulfed in shadow. Ava searched the main floor for anything out of the ordinary, taking her time examining everything in her immediate view. She took in a deep breath, sucking in the air to pick up any hint of fragrances from perfumes, deodorants, or fabric softeners. She took another deep breath. The air was still. The place smelled of metal and grease from the lack of circulation. Satisfied, Ava continued through the factory.

Ava crept through the south end of the factory where the majority of the milling, drilling, and boring had been done. Each of the metal machines was coated with a shade of paint that corresponded with the type of work that was done. Around each station on the floor, yellow lines with 'caution' or 'please do not touch' were written in bold letters. Blue arrows on the floor directed patrons through the factory to optimize their educational experience.

Dozens of stations were spread across the main floor, leading to the north side of the building which was dedicated to the equipment for the foundry. The northside housed the molds, tracks, and carts for raw material intake and distribution, and a giant ladle that was sectioned off from the rest of the foundry. The ladle hung close to the ceiling to avoid any possible mishaps from an overly tactile patron. In the very middle, a set of metal staircases led to a catwalk two and a half stories up that split the building in half. An "Excuse our dust" sign was placed in front of a long tarp that blocked the entrance to the elevator shaft that was left unfinished.

Ava scurried like an insect, darting from cover to cover, keeping herself concealed within their shadows. She ignored each one of the warning signs about touching the machines. *The building should be empty.* No one that she could remember saw her enter and she never hinted to the fact that this was going to be one of her destinations. But this night had been stuck in the realm of the unexpected. There was no point in throwing caution to the wind five steps from freedom.

Ava knew that even if a few had entered before her ward was started, she would still be fairly safe from the bulk of demons that may still roam the surrounding area. The ward encompassed the entirety of the building in a practically invisible bubble. Its formation used every bit of Greed and Envy that was left for the protective shield against any possible physical intrusion. Its shell should be strong enough to hold off any attack thrown its way for several hours at the very least. The ward was also created to hide her presence with the addition of a powerful fraud spell. The fraud spell was one of the strongest Ava had ever created in her life. It could convince all but the most powerful demons to search elsewhere for life. The entire process, creating the ward, and funneling energy into it took Ava several grueling days to complete.

Rhea was right. Ava did excel at fraud spells, but she came to that conclusion years ago when they were still traveling together. Since then, Ava has traveled on her own and learned quite a number of things. Traveling through the rings of the Abyss and the Earthly plane in between, Ava learned and developed new spells, seals, incantations, wards, sigils, and symbols throughout the seven deadly-sins spectra. Her skills bloomed like the stalks of a sheep-eater plant.

Ava continued her trek across the factory floor. Her legs burned from the continuous squatting. "Only for one night," she muttered. Any other day or any other circumstance, Ava would have packed it in and quit by now, or at the very least, sat down to take a long break. *That can't happen tonight.* Time was running out and she could not afford to be late. She had a date with the rising sun and its celestial schedule waits for no one.

Leaning against one of the tall boring machines, Ava stretched out her legs. After being on the other extreme for so long, they seemingly fought back, almost determined to stay in their painful position. After about a minute or two they begin to concede to her wishes. The quick stretch and release of pressure was much needed, but she did not waste time by reveling in the pleasure of it. Ava's head periodically peeped around corners looking for any kind of movement. Her dark brown eyes darted to-and-fro as she scanned the area.

She spotted them. A set of Greys walked two abreast towards her general direction, not speaking a single word. Her head and eyes lingered even though she knew it was dangerous. The two wiry men looked a little more grizzled than the average Grey she had walloped in the tavern earlier. *They must be close to their first descent.* Ava watched the two like a Barn Owl.

Their heads pivoted from side to side like a set of perimeter searchlights. They walked almost like they were being dragged along by a conveyor belt. Their steps were smooth enough to make an aristocrat from the Dark Ages jealous. Ava ducked back behind the bulky machinery, squatting deep. Her back pressed firmly against the cold metal. The muscles in her back tightened from the sudden chill.

Another fight is coming. She knew it, but it did not bring her any joy. She wanted this night to be over, but it would not stop. *If only they didn't see this building. I could have gotten to the top floor by now.* Ava peeked around the left side of the machine to watch the pair of Greys pass by oblivious to her presence. A smile crept to her face. Good news is good no matter how small. She was energized by the thought. Maybe it would be that easy.

If she crept low enough, she could sneak past those two men with no problem. Three hundred or so feet later she would be at the stairs. Then she could cross the catwalk, go through the worker's exit, and straight up to the backside of the restaurant. After that, release the main seal and…

A sharp noise from behind shook Ava out of her daydream. Her head spun around in its direction. Nothing was there but unused equipment and a few cobwebs. Their strands shimmered in the moonlight. The area was as still as it was when she crept by earlier.

Mere moments before Ava continued her voyage to the metal staircase, she heard the same noise again. The sound was like metal clanging against metal. Ava froze in place. Her ears perked up to hear any noise, no matter how low, that emanated around her.

"There you are."

Ava heard it in her ears and felt it in her chest. She rolled her eyes and then stood up, resigned to the fact that her time for sneaking was over. Her hands clenched into tight fists. A couple of her knuckles cracked from the force. With the excess energy from Gluttony, Ava was ready and able to meet any of the forces that were now trapped in the factory with her.

Two sets of Greys approached her position rapidly. One set came from the direction of the main entrance, pointing in her direction. The other set of Greys approached her from the left. Ava breathed a sigh of relief. She should be able to handle four Greys with relative ease. She smiled.

"She's right down there."

Ava's smile vanished and switched to a grimace. *I should have known.*

Six more Greys rushed across the catwalk like a squad of soldiers moving in double time. They must have been searching the other floors. *Would they have noticed?* Ava doubted it. The seal should have hidden it from their average prying eyes. Their stampeding feet clanged against the stairs as they made their way down to the first floor. Ava swallowed her disappointment. She had to do what she had to do.

Ava backpedaled into the main aisle of the floor, clearing herself of any obstacles that could be in her way. They closed in, forming a half circle. The Greys pulled out all manners of tools from their pockets; knives, brass knuckles, and a chain with a combination lock attached to the end.

The chain and lock took hold of her attention. *Where have I seen that before?* It was too bulky and heavy to be stuffed in a regular pocket without it busting through the seams and spilling to the floor. She remembered seeing locks like those during her high school years. Everyone bought the same combination lock with the dial for their lockers. It became a standard for high schooler's supplies. There was no real fear of items being stolen or the inside of lockers being vandalized.

The lock mainly gave the teenagers a sense of privacy which in turn helped them feel more like adults.

Seconds before the Greys leaped in for their attack, the emergency exit slammed open. That was when Ava knew. The familiarity of the lock and chain had nothing to do with her pivotal teenage years and the mandatory seven hours of public babysitting. The lock and chain were used to keep the rear door secure and to discourage the area's youth from sneaking into the building and smashing windows or doing any other sort of vandalism. Even in the heat of the situation, the irony was not lost on her. No longer a deterrent, the bulky chain would now be wielded by the Grey as a modern-day morning star to split her unprotected skull in two.

Her mind returned to the crashing of the emergency door. Through that exit, four more Greys rushed onto the main factory floor, breathing heavily. With the last of the Greys that streamed in, Ava had reached her quota. No matter how quickly she dispatched each one, she would be tired, injured, or both by the end of it. The deck was extremely stacked in their favor.

How many are left? Envy, Greed, and Gluttony have all been used up completely.

"We're only going to ask once." The lead Grey said, waving his switchblade around like a Westside Story Jet. "Where's the souls?"

They obviously haven't seen or heard about what happened in the tavern earlier or he wouldn't have asked such a stupid question.

The circle of Grey's constricted around her as they waited for her reply. Ava's answer did not matter to most of them. They were not there to collect anything. All they cared about, the ones in charge anyway, was a little bit of revenge or some sadistic fun. But, for anyone in the group that was more of the 'teacher's pet' type or 'by the book,' they could say, "We tried but she left us with no option. We had to beat it out of her."

Ava did not bother looking around at each one of them to see where they were in the circle or what they might be holding. Formulating a new plan had the utmost priority. She decided within a few seconds that she only had one good option.

Inside the tavern, the location gave her an advantage so she could take her time, but with the open factory floor, they could easily overwhelm her. *Strike first and finish quickly.* Once the first Grey stepped up, Ava put her plan into action. She attacked fast.

Punches and kicks that once knocked out each Grey she targeted with one or two hits now took four to five for the possibility of knocking them down. But they continued to get back to their feet on their own.

She doubled her efforts with her next set of strikes. Ava aimed at every vital point she could remember through the heat of the battle. But her mind was chaotic. Her thoughts were frantic, darting back and forth like a panicked fish. The few inner voices that remained bickered amongst themselves. Fear and dread spread like a contagion. The confidence that helped her power through two-thirds of the night had been slowly draining away. A stiff kick to her lower back knocked her off balance. She stumbled forward for a few steps before colliding with a fist.

Ava had let herself get surrounded while she was distracted. Her eyes squinted and watered from the pain. It hurt but not nearly as bad as what Nathan did to her. Seeing the once invincible Ava become suddenly vulnerable to damage excited the Greys and three rushed in for an attack. The chain was swung, punches and kicks were thrown, and two big meaty hands clutched at her body and clothes.

At the moment, Ava did not have as much power behind her attacks as she once had. Luckily for her, she still had some speed and could dodge fairly well. Either from her heightened instincts or their ill skills, the heavy metal chain that was meant to crash upon her face or wrap around her throat, careened over her head as she dropped down into a low squat. The heavy-duty chain collided with the tall Gray that rushed up from her side in hopes of grabbing her body, holding her in place. His arms flailed wildly from the pain as the chain crashed into his face, shattering his cheekbone. Blood oozed from his thin nose after the chain finished its journey around his face. The chain wielder stared dumbfounded. His colossal cohort collapsed backward with a gut-wrenching scream, landing on the ground with a wet slap.

The possibly fatal mistake caused an almost complete standstill from the remaining Greys. They were terrified deer staring down a set of headlights and Ava did not waste any time to attack. She knew she had to get hold of a weapon as quickly as possible. As she sprang back up from her squat, Ava tackled the chain wielder. Scooping him off his feet with both of her arms and her momentum. Her shoulder struck his solar plexus, knocking the wind out of him. He fell hard on the ground. His elbows hit first, trying in vain to brace himself from the impact. His head hit next, bouncing from the impact, leaving a splotch of blood on the sealed concrete like a freshly spilled splash of paint.

The attack snapped the Greys out of their collective stupor. The closest two struck with extreme ferocity at Ava who was still crouched over their fallen comrade. But in reality, Ava had not been there for quite some time. They had collectively been charmed with a fraud spell of her afterimage. The duo whacked at the unconscious Grey's body that lay before them.

Ava popped up in front of a few of them, the chain dangling at her side. With a quick motion, she lashed them across their faces and chests. They dropped their weapons and clutched at their injured body parts. The thrashed Greys collectively collapsed like bowling pins.

Ava looked up at the rest of the Greys. Their faces were stuck in shock from the events that transpired in the last few minutes. Five minutes later, their numbers had dwindled down to three. All except one was seemly stuck in fright.

The leather-clad old man that she had noticed standing at the edge of the catwalk, leapt from its height, landing in the middle of the crowd in a deep squat. The Greys stepped away in shock. Now that he was closer, she could tell that her first assessment of him was completely wrong. He was not a Grey. Ava could see that now. He was a Traveler. She could smell the brimstone on him. The 8-pointed star which was branded on the back of his hand, looked fresh. He must have been new.

How many levels has he passed through so far?

The Traveler was stout with a baby beer gut. His long sleeves were rolled up halfway up to just above his well-defined, hairy forearms. The mat of hair that burst from the top of his unbuttoned shirt matched the forest of hair that grew on his face. He looked strong. The kind of strength that came from years of hard labor on construction sites. The Traveler unstrapped his suspenders, letting them dangle at his sides.

Ava readied herself.

A shout from the distance, "laughing hyena," echoed through the factory.

-10-
RABENMUTTER

Ava's eyes drifted back up to the catwalk. A small figure approached the railing and leaned over, lightly stroking its metal. It was Betta, her Den Mother. *The fighting Fish.*

The Fighting Fish was the name Ava liked to call Betta behind her back whenever she was upset or felt like she had been wronged by her.

Rhea Kane took Ava to see Betta a few weeks after showing her the first spell she had ever learned.

"It's a simple charm that can relieve you of some of your burdens," Rhea said. After that, Ava wanted to know more and learn more. "That can only be taught by your Den Mother," Rhea said.

Ava prodded for answers but there was only one answer Rhea was willing to give, "She will tell you." It was always such a disappointing answer, but it did its intended job. Ava yearned to know more. And so, she agreed. She would go to meet this Den Mother and if the Den Mother saw fit, she would teach her the basics and maybe more.

"We're both Greys, but I won't be one soon," Rhea said, sitting at the end of a king-size mattress. The mint green sheets and covers were still tucked in neatly from the housekeeping that was done by the staff earlier that day. Ava fumbled through her suitcase that sat on the TV stand.

The two of them had been sharing a room at a motel a few miles outside of Boulder, Colorado for four days now and Ava was getting antsy. Since they started their weekend travels, Ava discovered her hidden wanderlust. She did not like to stay in one place for too long. Even in her hometown, Ava developed a never-ending thirst for the new and unexplored. Being in a city like Boulder for three days, or any place for that matter, felt like she was being trapped.

"I'm a what?"

"A Grey," Rhea reaffirmed.

Ava looked at the brown skin on the back of her hands. She pulled at her braided hair, showing it off to Rhea. "There's nothing Grey about me."

Rhea smiled. "Greys are new... er recruits."

Ava pouted and crinkled her nose.

"Don't look so… drab. Think of it like a sorority. Right now, we are pledges. To become a part of the sorority, you'll have to learn some tenets and complete some tasks. Easy." Rhea smiled.

"I'm from a small town, Rhea. We didn't have any sororities."

Rhea huffed. "I guess I'll have to explain then."

Ava smiled with delight and pulled up a chair. She plopped down in the wooden chair and placed her hands in her lap.

Rhea laughed. "Can you be serious for once?" She took a deep breath. "I'll tell you what I know. One of two people must find you, a Grey, or an Initiate. I was found by an Initiate. After they meet you and tell you a little about… their second life, they will test you… to see if you're interested in learning more—like a salesman."

Ava nodded like a first-grader. Her hands sat flat on her thighs.

"Cut it out," Rhea said. Her voice was sharp.

Ava stopped at once and sat up straight.

"At that moment you're a Grey. Not to say you weren't a Grey before that, everyone is. We just don't know it." She shook her head. "Stay on topic," Rhea said to herself. "The new Grey, which is you, is then introduced to a Den Mother. There are many Den Mothers, but I only know one. That's who you will meet today. The Den Mother teaches the basics and some of the advanced portions. The Den Mother will explain more about the process, and she will test the new Grey. She will also check to see if you are fit for the position. If you are… when you are—judged to be fit," Rhea said with a smile, "You will have a choice between two different tasks to complete. Then you can become a full member. I'm not supposed to tell you anything else."

"I'm still confused," Ava said.

"That's fine." Rhea tapped Ava on her closest leg beside her knee. "You're a smart girl," she smiled.

Ava blushed.

"And when you meet Betta," Rhea continued, "you will understand better. She's going to—"

"Betta? Like the fish?" Ava blurted out.

"Yes," Rhea said in a hushed tone. She looked around the room as if the eggshell-colored walls were leaning in for a quick bit of gossip. "And keep that to yourself. She might take offense."

Ava nodded. "I'm going to meet her today?" Ava said with excitement.

"We're going to make our way there right now." Rhea stood up and wrapped a wool scarf around her lean neck. She looked at Ava for a moment. "Please… don't embarrass us."

Ava stood and put the chair back. "You're the one that keeps telling me to talk more."

"You know exactly what I mean."

Forty minutes later, the duo arrived at Betta's home. It was a modest rancher with a manicured lawn and a silver ornate mailbox on a wooden post. Its red flag was raised, signaling that some mail was waiting inside. Ava followed Rhea into the house without a single question. Rhea did not knock or press a doorbell, she just turned the knob and walked right through.

In the basement, which had to be at the very least double the size of the house, they stood in front of a petite older woman who was a couple of inches shorter than both Rhea and Ava. The woman peered at them as they stood silent in the middle of a large room. Candles flickered on metal stands. The utility sink in the corner dripped from its rusty faucet. The air was cool and smelled of vanilla.

Ava never liked basements. They always reminded her of the weather that came sweeping through every year when she was young. Basements were always cold and sterile like those frigid nights. And the glow from the water heater that resided down in her parents' basement terrified her at night as a child. Its grill looked like the teeth of a terrifying monster. To her youthful mind, that crazed monster was always ready to spit fire at her if she ever dared to descend to its lair alone and in the dark.

The petite woman circled Ava, examining every inch of her. From head to toe, Betta studied Ava like a pretentious art dealer. Ava tracked the strange woman with her eyes but did not dare to move out of place.

Before walking into Betta's 'Den,' Rhea warned Ava for the last time. "Do not speak unless spoken to and please… keep all of your opinions to yourself. All right?" Ava listened to her friend and agreed without any objections. She wanted to be a part of whatever this was and if that meant being as obedient as a new military recruit, she would shower Betta with all of the 'yes Sirs', and 'no Sirs' that would be needed.

Ava looked down at the woman's small frame. Her arms held tight to her sides.

"Ava, I presume?"

Ava nodded.

"And do you know who I am, or—do we need introductions?"

Ava nodded halfway through Betta's questions.

"Which is it? And use your mouth this time," Betta said.

Ava looked over at Rhea before speaking. Rhea never changed her forward gaze. "I know who you are," Ava said.

"Do you?" Betta stopped in front of Ava. Her eyes shimmered from the candlelight. "Who am I?"

Ava hesitated. "You're a Den Mother." The words came out unsure.

"Yes, I am a Den Mother, but--there are plenty of those. Who am I?"

Ava looked back over at Rhea.

"Look. At. Me," Betta said sharply. "I am questioning you, not her."

Ava's head snapped back to its original position. Her heart was beating fast. Sweat started to form on her face and the back of her neck. "You're Betta," she said. "Like the fish." The words leapt out quicker than her mind could filter them. Ava gave a nervous smile. Her forehead was beaded with sweat.

A snarl crept onto Betta's face and then spread itself evenly into a smile. She took a deep breath. "Yes," she said. "Betta, like the fish. And do you know what I do?"

"You teach the Greys," Ava said. Her palms felt sweaty. She wanted to hide from the embarrassment.

"I teach. I train. I groom, I mold." Betta nodded. "A Den Mother nurtures its Greys under her wing, until—they're ready to leave the nest and travel on their own. But, to do that, each Grey must prove themselves. Did Rhea tell you how you might do such a thing?" Betta encircled the pair as she paced around the basement.

"No. She said it was your job to explain that." Ava at once tucked her lips and glanced at Rhea. She did it again. She spoke without thinking. Since becoming friends with Rhea, Ava's social habits have been returning to their previous standing before the incident. She was rash and impulsive. It had a sort of charm that seemed to work wonders for her back home in her tiny pond of a community. People loved her for it, especially the adults. But for the rest of the world, from what she could tell, her 'outbursts' were viewed as rude and uncultured behavior.

Rhea's eyes were set wide. She got a quick glimpse of Ava before her head was twisted in the opposite direction. The slap across Rhea's cheek echoed off the stone walls that surrounded them. Her pale face flushed, and her lips quivered. A split near the corner of her mouth released a spot of blood.

"Not in those exact words." The words hurried out of Ava's mouth. She tried her best to fix what she had mistakenly caused. "It was more like… you were better able to explain the process to me."

"I do know better." Betta lowered her hand. She stared at Rhea, who avoided her gaze. Rhea preferred to have a staring contest with the door handle on the other side of the room. "We do not bleed. Correct that."

Rhea's hands and fingers moved rapidly, forming a few basic magical gestures. After that, Rhea's face was back to normal. No bruise, no blood, and no cut. She looked the same as she did earlier that day.

"Good." Betta nodded with approval. She turned away from them, continuing her pace around the basement. "Before we get started, I will let you in on something important. There are only three paths to this life that you have been born into--and by following Rhea here today, you have already chosen yours. There's no backtracking or changing the course. You are now with us, and we are with you. From this day and until your death, you will climb down to the Abyss where you will find everything you ever wanted or needed."

Ava had so many questions, but she dared not ask them. Her mouth had gotten Rhea in too much trouble already. She did not want the repercussions to spill onto her.

"You will climb," Betta continued, "and you will learn." She turned and smiled like a friendly neighbor.

Erik McGowan

-11-
SLOTH

The last remaining Greys encircled Ava like a pack of hyenas, and she was the lone lioness who stumbled into their territory. With Betta's instructions, the group would become more organized.

The inner voices muttered and argued amongst themselves. Each one vying for their chance to fulfill their part of the bargain as soon as possible.

"Attack first. I'm ready," the voice growled. It was tired of sitting on the sidelines, watching everything from a distance. It wanted to be a part of the action like Envy and Greed.

"They will never touch you," another whispered. Its connection was weaker than the remaining few, but it was still there.

Each Grey took turns attacking Ava, one after another. They would launch a quick attack and then retreat to their starting position without hesitation. Ava knew the tactic. She knew it well. It was one of many that Betta taught her and Rhea. The tactic was also the initial attack pattern of the Hell Hounds. Betta had code names for everything. And like her name, the vast majority were named after animals.

"Symbols can hold more meaning than simple words. They can work as doublespeak. They can hide true meaning within their borders like the treasure inside of an ordinary box."

The attacks from the Greys did no damage but defending against them drained her energy.

"Great Ape," Betta shouted.

The biggest Grey jumped into the circle with both arms raised high over his head. He swung them down at the same time. His target was Ava's shoulders, right at the ends of her collarbones. The force would have caused severe muscle strains at her neck or even dislocated one or both of her shoulders.

Ava saw the Grey while he was still in the air. His legs kicked back like a spiking volleyball player. She stepped away at an angle from the Grey's swing, electing to dodge instead of wasting precious energy on blocking or deflecting.

"Cobra, constrict. Strike," Betta shouted. The circle collapsed to five feet in diameter. The head of the cobra, the stout Traveler, moved in from behind.

When Ava dodged the powerful hammer fist strike, she unwittingly moved herself just enough to also avoid the strike from behind. A punch whizzed past the side of her head, grazing her earlobe. In return, Ava's elbow slammed into the bridge of his nose. The Traveler stumbled back holding his bloody nose. She did not stop there. She delivered a snappy kick to his gut. The kick added to his backward momentum, and he stumbled into the Greys that surrounded them. They pushed him back into the fight like the tight ropes of a wrestling ring.

He rushed at her like a stampeding water buffalo. With his head low, the Traveler's arms were like the horns of the wild beast. Ava leapt over him. Using the bumbling Traveler's back as a springboard, Ava dropkicked the closest Grey in the chest and chin. The kicked Grey crashed down, sliding across the floor from the impact.

She sprang to her feet and rammed into the Traveler's exposed backside, shoulder first, as he tried to get to his feet like a toddler. He fell to the ground, arms and legs splayed like a starfish.

That old, out-of-shape, leather chaps-wearing Traveler was no trained fighter like Kismet or herself. He was more akin to an average street brawler. He had no skill in his attacks. He lacked the balance, speed, and awareness that any self-respecting fighter would have.

Was he really trained by Betta? Has she lost her killer instinct and consequently has been unable to pass down that mentality to her more recent pupils? Does she train men? All those thoughts ran through her head like an Olympic sprinter. Ava did not have an answer to either one of those questions. It never occurred to her to keep tabs on her Den Mother and her future pups. All the prepping in the world cannot prepare you for every possible outcome. And did it matter? If he was not trained properly, that would only add to the wins in her column.

Ava saw the arms before she felt them. The man-ape from earlier wrapped his muscular arms around her in a tight hug, pinning her arms under his own. With just the weight of his upper torso, he almost smothered her. Ava dropped her hips immediately to lower her center of gravity. He was a big burly guy, so her lowered stance made it harder for him to lift her without changing his position first.

Ava took full advantage of his delay. She grabbed his exposed thumb on the hand he was using to support his grip. With a sharp twist, Ava broke his grip and his thumb. He clenched his teeth from the pain. A quick back kick to his family jewels convinced him to release her. He cupped his damaged member instead. The brute fell to the ground, rolling in pain. He cursed her and her parents as the intense pain flowed through the rest of his body.

The two Greys that made up the now semi-circle stood in place, seemingly waiting for another command that did not come.

Did I finally shut you up Betta? Ava smiled.

Each part of Ava's body began to feel heavy. The weight hung off her as she moved, making each movement much more labor-intensive. Her legs felt like they were stuck in tar. Her shoulders and neck bowed towards the ground. Her clothes felt like lead. She felt like a chained animal, struggling to break free, but she could not escape their constraints. Had her fatigue finally caught up to her? Ava's legs quivered after every few steps. It was as if that huge bulk of a man was still wrapped around her like a weighted straight jacket. The Greys smiled as she expelled large amounts of energy trying to reach them. They danced out of range to Ava's frustration. They knew something, but she did not know what. Gluttony was gone. Its voice had been silenced. There was no way to rejuvenate herself anymore.

Something was wrong. Her positive momentum was now slipping away. If she could not keep up, Ava would bring them down to her. "Veternus," she commanded. Hidden beneath her jeans, the tattoos on her legs spun like a centrifuge. The band on her calf could partially be seen through the holes that were left by the Hell Hound's bite. Sloth's influence radiated from her. Waves of Sloth rushed outward, crashing against the last three men and whatever else that may be around hiding on the factory floor.

Sloth did not speed Ava up, nor did it transfer power over to her like Greed or Envy. It washed over the area with weakness and a lethargic energy. The three attackers slowed. Their movements became clumsy. The weight that was holding Ava down and keeping her from moving at her accelerated pace eased. After a few moments, the unexplained weight left her suddenly and completely. She felt new.

And then she noticed something near her shoulder. Its pudgy face appeared to be peering over her shoulder like a nosy child. She swatted at it. Ava watched as a couple of Ushi-oni dropped off her body like ripe walnuts. Fat and plump, the Ushi-oni broke apart like fragile stones after hitting the ground.

She could now see that a few Ushi-oni held tight to the bearded Traveler's body like the molted carcasses of an insect. Their giant bug eyes drifted closed like an easy-going garage door before they fell from their host like ripened fruit from its branch. The Traveler looked at the comatose creatures. His lips curled at the sight of their speckled bodies. He kicked one across the factory floor like a soccer ball. Its tiny body rammed against one of the drilling machines. A purplish paste marked its impact. Its body did not move, and its eyes did not open from the pain.

Some of the Ushi-oni were piled on top of the giant Grey who continued to cry out while cradling his testicles. A few of those Ushi-oni that had clung to her, weighing her down like a diving belt. Their now unconscious bodies lay motionless around her feet. When did it start? That did not matter. One Traveler and two more Greys left, and then Betta.

Sloth worked on the remaining three as well as it did in the tavern. With each invisible wave that emanated from Ava, the three combatants' speed, strength, and even their thoughts failed them in little increments.

Sloth's voice was panicked. "The others. I can see them."

The Others had finally found Sloth somewhere in the Abyss. Soon, the torture would begin. It was an inevitability. All the souls knew that from the moment they met Ava and agreed to her request.

"Please," the voice cried. "No."

Sloth was reaching its limits. No more waiting for an opening. It was now or never, or Ava would have to switch tactics. But what would that leave for Betta?

Ava looked up, catching Betta's eye. She had been watching the whole thing. Betta might know about Sloth, but maybe not the remaining souls. The three approached at opposite angles, as swiftly as they could arrange. Their speed dropped down to an average person. Their power was gone. Without their physical prowess and the Ushi-oni used to drag down their victims, they were nothing. Two quick defections were followed up with a stiff roundhouse kick to the side of the neck, a sharp knee to the sternum, and a quick punch to the face.

Their bodies shut down before they collapsed to the ground. Ava looked back up to Betta to see her reaction. She wanted to see disgust or disappointment on her face. Ava would relish the sight. To see the legendary Betta's face in shock, knowing full well that her time was coming, and she would share the same fate as all of her subordinates, would put her over the moon. Alas, Ava saw none of that. Much like

Nathan standing on top of that hill, she could not read Betta's face at all. If Betta was worried or in the throes of panic, she did not show any signs of it.

That only meant that Ava would have to show her why she should feel threatened. Ava was not the same woman Betta had trained all those years past. She was going to climb those stairs and make her see the reality of her situation. Ava had stood toe to toe with the Lord of Violence and survived. The Fighting Fish would be no real obstacle.

This night had been challenging, but with those challenges, Ava was pushed harder than she had ever been before in her life. She looked at the stairs and then back at Betta.

I'm coming for you.

-12-
ENVY

Ava sprinted to the top of the catwalk, disregarding her stamina. She skipped every other step as she made her way up to her Den Mother. The metal rang as she climbed. Ava stopped five feet from Betta who stood between her and the stairwell. The fatigue that was one or two steps behind Ava as she made her ascent caught up with her moments after she stopped.

The two old acquaintances were like two cowboys at high noon, staring each other down to see who would break first. Ava clenched her jaw. She expelled air out of her mouth with each exhale. Her mouth ballooned from the force of the air. Her hands fidgeted by her side, ready to draw her 'weapons' at any moment.

Gluttony, Sloth, Greed, Envy. Ava counted to herself. *They're all gone. Sloth could have been helpful, but Betta had been watching the fight. She would have known what I was doing before it had a chance to work. What can I do?* Ava took a few more steps forward.

"Breathe," Betta said, comfortable in her position.

Betta's voice brought back an intense flood of memories. Eighteen long months of intense training and torturous disciplines. Endless days and sleepless nights filled with blood, gallons of sweat, and rusty buckets of salty tears.

Ava took in that much-needed deep breath. Her nose flared as she filled her lungs up to its full capacity. *Breathe… I know to breathe.* Her face was infused with a deep disgust. *Still telling me what to do.*

Betta smirked. "Very good."

Those last two words felt like a pat on the head from a proud parent or mentor. The sentiment disarmed Ava for only a moment, but that moment was long enough. Betta had crushed plenty of opponents within momentary lapses such as this one, hundreds of times. Betta leapt towards Ava with a flurry of attacks. With her fingertips pressed together like the beak of a bird, Betta attacked Ava with White Crane Gung-Fu. Betta's movements flowed like a thin cloth in a calm wind. Her strikes were quick and snappy like that same garment struck by a strong gale.

If Only For One Night

The attacks were precise, but her timing was like a staggering drunkard. The moments between movements looked as though there were several openings to exploit. There seemed to be some small chance for Ava to counter with an attack of her own, but within a fraction of a second Betta would move into her next attack. All Ava could do was back away, dodge, or block Betta's well-honed attacks.

Few more hours left…if that. Ava's night was almost over. She came so close to slipping past Betta with several types of feints and then making a break for the metal door. She would dash up the stairs and complete her task before Betta could catch up. But nothing she tried was working. When she sidestepped, Betta was there to block her path. Ava tried to leap over her old Den Mother's head, but Betta struck at her legs, stopping her before she could finish getting her legs ready for the jump.

Ava was trapped within her assault and backed into a corner. The catwalk's stairs were her only good means of escape. That route took her away from where she really needed to go, which was either around or through the Fighting Fish. Ava took another step back. Her heel slapped against the brick wall behind her.

Betta stopped at once and stepped back a few paces. "Your turn." She winked.

My turn? She's treating this like some sparring session. Ava went on the attack. Kicks and punches were thrown at Betta with all the force and speed she could muster. Ava would not be able to keep up the pace for long, but if any of her strikes were to hit their target, she would not need to. Saying that Ava weighed seventy pounds more than Betta would be generous. Every hook, jab, roundhouse kick, sidekick, and straight punch was answered with a decisive strike from Betta. With every missed blow, Ava received pain in return. With every blocked attack, Ava's body stung like it was whacked by a freshly cut switch. Betta stayed close enough to strike but far enough to avoid Ava's attacks with low effort.

Ava's joints ached from Betta's counterstrikes. She wanted to stop, but she could not. She dared not. Ava had to believe that one of her attacks was bound to land and lead to a change in the fight. *No one is perfect forever. Betta will make a mistake. Her timing will falter. It has to happen.*

Ava continued to advance with attacks and the Den Mother backpedaled in kind, poking at her openings like a world-class fencer. She punished Ava for every mistake and missed opportunity. The brawl was a game of cat and mouse where the cat had no claws, its teeth were dull, and it was malnourished.

The whole situation was maddening, and infuriating. Even with all of her training throughout the levels of the Abyss and the research she had done over the years on her own, Ava was still being taught a lesson. Pride had crept forward once again, sinking its tentacles deeper into her foundation.

Why? She screamed internally. *Why?* Ava lunged at Betta's small frame with both hands extended like a pro wrestler. She was frustrated. She was desperate. Ava wanted more than anything to get her hands around Betta's scrawny neck and choke every last bit of life out of her. She wanted to watch as Betta's face transitioned from scarlet to a deep purple as she tried her best to get a sip of air. Killing any member from the Abyss, no matter how gratifying it would be, would only add more debt to Ava's already substantial amount of time. But, to get those few minutes of seeing the fear and pain in Betta's glassy eyes before her life was snuffed out, would be well worth it.

Ava's desperate gambit fell far short of any kind of payoff. Betta sidestepped Ava's attempt to capture her. She struck out at Ava's unguarded back. Betta's finger jab hit its intended target, Ava's exposed spine, right between her shoulder blades. Her attack was the same technique that Kismet attempted earlier and barely missed. A sharp pain shot through her entire back. All of the muscle groups that surrounded her spine seized like a dry engine. Ava stumbled forward from the force. Her arms flailed as she tried to find some sort of balance or something to hold onto to keep herself upright. The catwalk rushed towards her like a speeding train. Seconds before having a meeting between the metal grating and her face, Ava was yanked up by the back of her neck and lifted off her feet. She hung in place as limp as a kitten in the jaws of their parent.

Ava gasped, reaching for the hand that held her tight. The invisible force launched her into the nearby office, crashing through the plexiglass barrier that protected the props, barely missing the metal desk's sharp edges. Her head rang against the metal wall. The mock inventory papers fluttered in the air like a flock of scared birds. Ava's thoughts collided with one another like atoms in a fission reactor.

"Now we're even." Rhea Kane appeared in the doorway. The pale moonlight outlined her thin figure through her wispy linens. Her facial features were barely visible through the shadow that was cast.

Ava lay crumpled like Rhea's unconscious body did at the tavern. The world swirled in Ava's eyes. It was a whirlpool of light. She blinked in slow motion. The office was now a moon bounce with overly energetic children in it. No matter how hard she tried, Ava could not get her balance. Her hands fumbled around the floor, searching for some stability. Her legs would not move in the proper direction. She tried to stand but her thoughts were too mixed up to coordinate her limbs properly.

"Why didn't you give them up?" Rhea shook her head. "Why?" A hint of sorrow lingered in her voice.

Ava struggled to speak. She could understand the questions, but she could not string together the proper responses. Her mind was jumbled, tumbling like clothes in a dryer. "Sack… Sack of ice. Free. Leave on." She blinked a few times to get her bearings, but her lips and tongue kept failing her. *Levi.*

"You knew the rules, Ava." Rhea snarled. "Nothing is free. We all had to make sacrifices. All of us." She reached into the room and hit the light switch. A bulb, dangling in the center of the room, turned on. Its light barely pierced through its dusty glass covering. Rhea's eyes grew sad, giving way to everything that twisted and turned under the surface. "The moon is on high, baby girl." Rhea pointed at the Moon. It hung over the Factory's skylight like an enormous disco ball. "Capatus furem (Shadow Demons)," she almost whispered. The words filled up the room like a shout into an echo chamber, ricocheting off the metal container's walls. "They will take you back to the Abyss. So long Ava." She paused. "This is where we part."

Rhea yanked on the door, sliding it closed with a clang. Then came the sound of scraping metal, as Rhea closed the latch, locking the office's door from the outside. The light bulb that hung from the ceiling rocked back and forth like a pendulum. The shadows rocked in time with the motion of the light. Ava's heavy eyes stared at the rusted door as the shadows did their rhythmic dance. Her fingers feebly scraped at the thin rug that covered most of the floor. It was all she could manage. She was too weak to stand or even crawl. If she were to mistakenly tip herself over, Ava had no confidence in her ability to prop herself back up.

Ava wheezed. Her head hung low to her chest, making it harder for her to breathe. The back of her head felt damp. Was it from the impact or all the sweat? She had been sweating again since the fight with Betta and the Greys but when she crashed into the wall, her head hit hard. Her body ached all over from injuries and exhaustion. All of it was too much for her to handle.

I need a break. She blinked. *That's all. A quick break.* She blinked again. Her eyelids stayed closed for a couple of seconds longer. *Five minutes... and I'll be...*

Ava's eyes drifted shut.

-13-
NO LIGHT

The exhausted mind often becomes the playground for its unconscious brother who spends most of its time reveling in the past. Ava could no longer hold back those mental demons that pushed her pain and suffering back to the forefront.

There was a blur of movement and a flash of light.

Ava blinked rapidly. Her face ached and burned. The pain intensified with every passing second. Her eyes watered but refused to overflow. The extreme pain muscled its way passed her confused thoughts. Her hand slapped against the side of her face as she tried to seize the pain within her grip and sling it far away. The side of her face was wet with a warm viscous liquid. The burning sensation grew worse the longer her hand lingered. The sensation was worse than all the needles she had received from the shaky dentist assistant who administered anesthesia into her gums for a root canal on her lower molar. It felt like a hot rod was placed on the side of her face that slowly increased in temperature.

Ava pulled her hand away. She looked at it in the dim orangish-tinted streetlight. The amber liquid converted her palm into a bloody Rorschach test. Even though the color was wrong, Ava knew exactly what it was. She was bleeding, but what she could not figure out was why and when did it start.

Ava's mind zipped back to earlier that day. She remembered being in the park, spending most of her time sitting on a park bench, soaking up the warm sun rays. She watched the different people who walked by on their way to who-knows-where. She was so caught up in her musings over her surroundings, that Ava hardly ate any of the lunch that was packed for her by her mother. The paper bag of food sat on the park bench beside her like a placeholder to keep strangers away.

Dusk approached as time flew along like a lofty pigeon. Foot traffic declined with the setting Sun. Clouds crept overhead at a snail's pace. Ava made her way out of the park, following the deserted footpaths to the main street. She let too much time escape her and she needed to make it back to the hotel. The chaperones, Mrs. Jackey and Mrs. Turner were both bound to be worried if they had known Ava had not been back yet.

After exiting the park, Ava heard someone cry out. She looked up and down the street in search of its point of origin and its attended target. The streets were busy with traffic, but the sidewalks were as vacant as the park. She heard the voice again, this time more distinct and from behind. She whipped around on her heels to see a young man exiting the park.

He spoke. Ava could not remember his exact words, but she had not forgotten his voice. It had a gritty, guttural sound like he smoked at least two packs a day and yet somehow smooth at the same time. Or maybe the silkiness of his words was more about how they were said and how they seemed to bounce along the air to her ears. Gentle words and compliments poured out of his mouth as he smiled. His words were as fast as the big city that they were in, and his slang was as flashy as his colorful outfit and expensive jewelry. His gold timepiece glittered as he spoke. The single initial that hung from his Cuban link chain danced as he swayed.

The conversation switched from the initial pleasantries to the more intimate, 'getting to know each other better', type. After his five-minute windup and hearing his skillful pitch, Ava gave a polite refusal to his invitation, but the young man was persistent. He moved closer as he tried to reason with her. He touched her hand and rubbed her exposed shoulder. Ava did not like the physicality of his courting, but she did not outright dislike it either. Once again, Ava turned him down, shaking her head while smiling.

Ava turned to walk away. It was getting darker by the minute, and she had to make it back to her hotel room. The young man stepped in front of her, unwilling to give up his pursuit. His hazel eyes were fierce now. His lips curled as he spoke. He demanded to know why she was refusing him. Ava told him with no hesitation. Since she was not from the area and even if she came back next year, she probably would not see him again.

He became furious. Apparently, he did not believe what she had said. Ava had seen and heard enough. Even if their paths had been destined to cross sometime in their foreseeable futures, her interest in him was no more. And with that, there was no reason to continue the conversation. He had become extremely rude and that was something she could not let continue. She stepped to the side to cross the street. He blocked her exit once again.

Ava looked around for any onlookers as she pleaded with him to stand aside. His words continued to be as venomous as a stonefish. Her heart rattled in her chest. Ava tried to push him out of the way, but her strength could not compete with his bulk. She felt small. He towered over her. His once appealing height and build now looked menacing in her nervous eyes. He shouted allegations and accused her of being stuck up, berating her with all manner of curses.

Ava franticly searched the block again for someone, anyone, but not a single soul was around. None of the cars that passed by on their way to their destination stopped to investigate. She was on her own and she was terrified. Her heart vibrated next to her gasping lungs. Ava tried her best to stay composed. Then she noticed a quick motion out the corner of her eye and felt a burning sensation course down the side of her face. She reached up and felt the blood.

Ava looked up from her bloody hand to the man that loomed over her. Tears blurred her vision. His face held no answer for what had just happened. He grinned with satisfaction and a hint of accomplishment. The next moment, Ava was on the ground covering up her damaged face, wailing into the night. The young man had pushed her to the ground with tremendous force and then—walked off.

That image stuck with Ava for many years later. He not only attacked her with no apprehension but then sauntered off like his heinous actions were an everyday occurrence. It was as if she somehow deserved what she got, and he had an obligation to fulfill the action. After Ava's assailant was several blocks away, someone finally came to her rescue. A woman found Ava on the sidewalk, face dripping with blood, balled up in the fetal position. The good Samaritan was on a late bike ride when she heard someone scream from several blocks away. The woman hailed a cab, helped Ava into the back of it, and followed her to the nearby hospital.

That night, the ER doctor and nurses told Ava that she was lucky not to have any permanent nerve damage as they cleaned the knife wound and stitched it up with a non-absorbable suture. The police officers that followed up about the park incident, remarked on how lucky she was to make it out of a situation like that with her life intact. Even her athletic savior said how lucky she was and how she normally did not ride that route late in the evening because of the muggings that had been occurring in that area over the past few months. Everyone seemed to think Ava was lucky except for the one whose opinion should matter, her own.

She was not lucky. It was the worst thing to ever happen to her and no one seemed to understand that. Her parents were no different. They did not care about how she felt. They talked about how she should not have been out on her own and how big cities are filled with nothing but crime. They tried their best to guilt-trip Ava over what might have happened if she had not been saved by the cyclist.

"What would we tell your brother?" Her mother said. "He's already going through a lot as it is."

Her father agreed. "You should have never been on your own at that time of night."

Growing up, Ava had spent many days out at night, alone, walking around her town. Doing the same in another city in Montana did not register as risky behavior. People were friendly where she lived, why would things be different anywhere else in the state? Her parents warned her of the big cities on the coasts, but the Midwest was always talked about like the Garden of Eden.

The officers had told Ava that she had been one of the many to be assaulted in a similar fashion within recent months. They called the attack a "buck-fifty." A street term for the assault because of the number of stitches or staples the victim would need to close their wound. They questioned her for an hour to get a better understanding of the incident and any description of her assailant she could come up with. Ava could not give them much. She could not remember the looks of her attacker and she did not want to. His face remained a blurry splotch in her memory. Her heart raced whenever her mind went back to that day, and her anxiety grew worse when she tried to picture his face.

One month after the incident, Ava's parents sent her back to school. Ava clung to her bookbag like a shield, holding it tight to her chest. Once an extrovert who loved to learn and to speak to almost everyone in the hallways, now, Ava was an introverted loner who hid her face from curious eyes. All of her extracurricular activities fell to the waste side. She stopped talking to her friends and rarely showed up to the bulk of her classes.

After her first day of school, Ava insisted on wearing long braids that hung over her face like a beaded curtain. Even with that covering, Ava could still feel her peers' eyes trying to pierce the veil of hair. She could hear the whispers amongst the other students, the taunts, the name-calling, and all of the degrading jokes about her on those twenty-minute bus rides. At first, Ava believed that the bus driver would notice the commotion and put an end to the harassment, but the woman never did turn around or reprimand the students. She was alone, every single day, in the midst of her tormentors.

A few times a week, the assistant principal and counselor would ask probing questions about her mental health, but never directly. They would continuously try to analyze Ava's emotional state, but she would give them nothing as usual. Ava would stare blankly at the floor in their office or out of a window until they gave up all hope for a breakthrough. After a few of those unproductive visits, the faculty seemed to collectively turn their attention to her parents; whispering and laughing.

Ava screamed inside. She did not want anyone to know what was going on with her or what she had gone through. It was none of their business. The story was hers and she did not want it to be told. But she knew. She knew they were blabbing about her and her stitched, damaged, ugly face. She knew they were laughing at her and telling all her secrets during their lunch breaks.

Her parents probably told them about how she would often wake up in the middle of the night, dripping with sweat, screaming like a banshee. Every single night, Ava's dreams were nothing but nightmares. At times those nightmares involved Ava being chased by some mysterious figure with no body. That shadowy apparition would race after her. It was always a few steps behind, no matter how fast she ran. No matter where she would try to hide, it would be there once she turned her head. Other times she would be boxed in with her back pressed flat against some wall and that same shadowy figure would loom over her with a jagged knife that did a terrifying dance in its hands before the inevitable strike. No matter how courageous she tried to be, the nightmares continued to happen.

Her parents probably talked about how she hid her face from them, even at home, preferring to eat alone in her room. Ava would take her plate up to her room where she would eat her meal in her bed with the light off and her door cracked to let in just enough light to see what she was eating. Even her brother was not allowed to see her without being covered up.

Or maybe they talked about how she had urinated on herself after being left alone with a tall male doctor for a few minutes as he tried to check her face. She shivered like a scared puppy in the back seat all the way back home. Once she got home, she spent hours on end in her washroom cleaning herself repeatedly.

They were telling them everything and she knew it. She was as certain as a Midwestern cold snap. Ava cursed the school staff in her head every time she would see them talking in between periods with hushed voices. Her heart would pound with hatred and then her face would ache with a brush fire from her temple to her chin.

Ava kept her head down and continued with her routine through the rest of the year. She came to school, sat alone in the corner of each class, did enough work to pass, ate her lunch alone with one arm guarding her face, and kept her mouth closed to everyone including her oldest friends. She continued to wear the gauze over her scar months after the stitches were taken out. Ava did not want anyone to see the patchwork of her two-toned skin that traversed the left side of her face, not even her family. People loved to gossip and with a population that was slightly under two thousand, rumors had a habit of spreading like cancer throughout Red Glen.

When ostracizing herself did not work and the whispers and ridicule continued, Ava started skipping school. She would take the school bus like normal while her mother watched from the yard, but when they arrived, she would never go in. The high school's entrance was always as busy as a buzzing beehive in the mornings which made it easier for Ava to promptly walk off in the opposite direction amongst the confusion.

Ava did not walk back to her neighborhood, risking her truancy being exposed to her parents, and she did not want to go to class and be stared at or asked a million questions about what happened by her peers. Instead, Ava would sit at the top of the football field's bleachers on its concrete steps. With her back slouched low against its wall to avoid detection, Ava would rub her aching face and wish with every fiber of her being that she could somehow change her past. Every night before falling asleep with a face full of tears, Ava desperately hoped she would wake up from that terrible existence and everything would be back to normal; back to the way things were five months ago.

After a few days, Ava's parents found out about her skipping school. Living in such a small town, Ava's parents were bound to bump into one of the school's faculty sooner or later. For the rest of that school year, both of her parents took turns personally taking Ava to school. They would sit through some of her classes to make sure she did not leave once they dropped her off. Their good intentions only made her academic life worse in the eyes of a young Ava. Their presence only added to the murmurs of the other students.

Starting mid-summer after her junior year, Ava began to escape into the world. On weekends, Ava would wake up at first dawn and escape into the nearby woods for hours on end, only to make her way back home well after dusk. Her hatred for all of the pretenders and gossipers that flooded her town burned like a metallurgical furnace until she breached the borders of the town and escaped into the world beyond. Years later she would learn about the term, wanderlust.

Sometimes those trips would lead her to the North Forks River where she would follow its banks south to the old miner's town. She would walk around its deserted boundaries muttering and making plans for a future away from Montana and everyone she had ever known.

At first, her parents panicked and called up the local Sheriff to find their missing daughter. He would find her within a few hours near Bearing or Klink and drive the wandering teen back home. But that did not deter Ava from widening her wandering distance and the amount of time away. After a while, the local shop owners would keep an eye out for Ava and report her whereabouts to law enforcement if she was spotted without at least one of her parents.

Ava's parents tried their best to reprimand her, but it did not work. No matter how much they took from her or grounded her, she would always make her escape. Talking was not helping and scolding her only seemed to accelerate the process. Ava treated her parents the same way she treated all of those nosy adults who tried to peer into her mind. She shut them out just as quickly. After two months of failed attempts to convince Ava to listen to reason, her parents decided to follow the suggestion of her high school counselor. At the end of August, right before the new school year, her parents took Avalee to see a professional therapist.

***

"Hi, my name's Rhea."

Ava looked up to see a young woman standing in front of her. She was the physical opposite of Ava. Rhea was pale, almost ghostly, with ocean-blue eyes and burgundy hair. She was thin. As thin as the runway models that sauntered down the catwalk in experimental designer clothing. Rhea's body also reminded Ava of the cheerleaders at her high school. They were always obsessing over how much they weighed. Rhea's clothes were loose and flowing, with different plants like ferns, ivy, and an array of flowers on each garment. The letter 'R' was embroidered near her collar. It stood out from the rest of her outfit like a freshly picked orange in a basket full of brown leaves.

"Hi," Ava stuttered as she caught a glimpse of Rhea's eyes. She was drawn to the deep blueness of them. It reminded her of the sea. She could feel herself being caught up in their currents.

Rhea smiled. The smile helped alleviate the tension that had built up in Ava over the past year. She could feel her muscles relax. Rhea sat down on the bench next to Ava. "I've seen you around here. Do you always come by yourself?"

Ava sat at a picnic table near the local bus terminal on the far end of its bench. Its wood was cracked and split from the many years of freezing and thawing without any paint to protect it from the elements.

Ava would travel there for a few hours a day after school, dreaming about how she would escape from her miserable small-town life. One day she would get enough courage to buy one of those one-way out-of-state tickets and ride out of town for the last time. Time was marching its way closer to her 18th birthday and with that came adulthood and her freedom, at least in the eyes of the courts.

Ava nodded, keeping her head low. She did not quite know what to say. Ava did not want to talk too much but she also did not want Rhea to leave. For some odd reason, she did not mind Rhea's company like she did everyone else. The return to normalcy gnawed at the back of her brain, even if staying secluded was not considered normal to most people. Ava had become used to the solitude, but now for some odd reason, she was torn.

"What's your name?" Rhea asked.

"Avalee."

"I'm sorry, I couldn't hear you." Rhea leaned in closer. The top half of her body breached the invisible line that separated Ava's personal space from everyone else's.

Ava looked up and was drawn back into Rhea's gaze. The view was pleasant. A smile tugged at the corners of her mouth, but Ava stopped it before it could fully divulge her feelings. She took a deep breath before speaking. "My name is Ava."

Ava saw Rhea's eyes shifting down to the gauze that covered her grotesque scar. She quickly tilted her head back down hoping Rhea did not get a good enough view or that she would take the hint and avoid asking any questions.

"That's why," Rhea said. She gave a sympathetic smile. "Hiding from the world?" She lightly jabbed Ava with her elbow. "You're too pretty for that."

Normally Ava would have had her face covered with a cotton mask and blamed it on being sick. That way she could say something about not wanting to spread her germs and that would be enough. Most people did not want to risk getting sick and when you were courteous enough to keep the germs to yourself, they would respect the civility and leave the person alone with no more questions. There were rare individuals over these last few months who would ask her follow-up questions about her sickness or would talk about their personal experiences. Some would try to give her their home remedies for all kinds of diseases, continuing the conversation that was unwanted from the start. In times like that, Ava would just fake a coughing fit, apologize in between hacks, and walk away.

For the past week, Ava had left her mask at home. People in other towns had not been fixating on her face as much as she had thought they might. The anxiety of it all was causing ulcers and more pain than before. Ava needed a change and that was her first step. Her next one would come after her birthday.

"What happened? Car accident? Or an alcoholic parent?" Rhea probed.

"Huh," Ava said. Her mind was still wrapped around the compliment. When was the last time someone really acknowledged her? "No, no, no." She shook her head at the idea. "It was a car accident." Her eyes drifted back down to the table. She did not want to let her eyes linger for too long.

"I had an accident too. I was young. Mine involved a bottle or two of bourbon and an agitated matriarch. I was in the hospital for a couple of months. Maybe one day we can compare scars." She smiled. The story was tragic, but Rhea's voice was as sweet as a honeydew.

Ava smiled at the idea even though the circumstances would have been quite dreadful two weeks ago. The fact that Rhea now knew about her scar did not fill Ava with any dread. She was not nervous or scared. She was oddly calm about the situation. It was a calm she had not felt in a very long time. Hours after their chance meeting, Ava would think long and hard about that.

The last time had to have been when Ava saw her baby brother for the very first time. She felt a connection with that sleeping baby that she had never felt before, from anyone, until now. Ava decided right then and there to give Rhea a shot. A real shot. Ava blurted out, "Want to be friends?"

Rhea wrapped her arm around Ava's shoulder and gave a quick squeeze. Ava felt warm, like a cup of hot chocolate at a ski lodge during a frigid winter's night. All of her insecurities melted away with the burst of warmth. After that hug, the world seemed new. Her dull day grew bright with the hope of the future.

Erik McGowan

Rhea said with a bright smile, "Sure. I would love that."

-14-
IF ONLY FOR ONE NIGHT

"What has gotten into you?" Ava's father shouted, but the words did not get through. They bounced off Ava's stony exterior like screams off a brick wall.

Ava's mother sat at the kitchen table, whaling. Her father stood next to his wife, rubbing her trembling back with his large hands.

Ava stood silent in the wide door frame of the kitchen. Her suitcase, filled with a modest amount of clothes and two pairs of shoes, sat on the floor by her feet. The bookbag she once used as a protective barrier through the second half of her high school years hung off her shoulder by one strap. A devious smile bubbled just under the surface. *Now they care.* Ava had been past the point of caring about their feelings for what seemed like a long time now and her mother's pitiful crocodile tears would not be enough to convince her to turn around.

"Why are you doing this to your family?" Her father said.

What about your little brother?" Her mother said through bouts of tears.

Ava had not thought about him. Throughout all the weeks of planning, prepping, dreaming, and planning some more, he did not cross her mind once and she must not have crossed his either. Neither one of the siblings had tried to communicate with the other for over a month. Rhea Kane and the promise of her new future, on her own, away from all these people, solely held her attention.

What was the reason behind them not talking? She could not remember. It could not have been something he did. He was as innocent as a brand-new baby bird. Ava could not think of a single time when he had ever made her upset or caused her to lash out.

What about your little brother? The question repeated in her mind.

Before the incident, Ava would hear her parents talking about him. They would have a full-blown conversation about his muteness as if he were not in the same room, playing with his toy or doodling in his coloring book. Those two talked about him as if he were a malfunctioning appliance that needed a quick repair. Those conversations were always about him, but they did not take the time to talk to him.

After the park incident, Ava and her brother seemed to switch places overnight. Ava became reluctant to speak and the new family pariah to be endlessly spoken about. Her little brother Levi became expressive. When he talked, though it was only a few words at a time, he sounded like he had been practicing for years on end.

Everyone that wanted her to talk, childhood friends, family, and the authorities only wanted to ask questions. Too many questions. They wanted to talk about her and at her but never with her. All Ava wanted was some peace and quiet. To be left alone was all she asked for. Silence and solitude had suited her better than the constant prying and digging.

They didn't care about Levi until he started to talk. I've always looked after him.

So, the pleas from her father which included the questions about her newfound selfishness and her lack of interaction with the family did not hold any weight in her eyes. Ava was tired of standing still, living an average small-town life. No matter how popular she could get or would have gotten in their wannabe city, her life would be nothing but average.

Ava had finally found something she did not know she was searching for and others to show her how to get more of it. Sticking around in that small-town dump stopped being a possibility for her months before Rhea showed up in her life.

"What about him?" Ava said. Her voice was dry. She sounded uninterested in the proposed question, but her mind was still pondering away. It latched on to that question for a couple of longing heartbeats.

What about him? The image of little Levi standing in front of her popped into her head.

On Ava's first night home from the hospital, she lay in her bed, curled up under her sheets, crying in silence. There was a light tap on her shoulder. She twitched from the unexpected touch. Earlier that day, she locked her door and stayed in her room sobbing, only to leave out to use the washroom. Ava had not heard the doorknob turn or the creak of the door opening, just that light touch. Ava wiped her face before turning over.

She poked her head out of the covers like a turtle checking its surroundings. Levi stood in front of her in his astronaut pajamas, with the same blank expression that he had worn for most of his life. She looked over at the alarm clock on her nightstand, 10:20 pm glowed on its surface. That was more than two hours past Levi's bedtime. *What was he doing out of bed?* Ava did not want to cry in front of him but the brief startle she had was beginning to wear off and the tears were making their way back. They gushed forth, spilling over the rims of her eyelids.

Levi gently caressed her cheek. It was one of the gestures that Ava would do when Levi appeared to be frustrated from not being understood. She would lightly rub his cheek and whisper, "It's going to be ok." Sometimes she would just pull him in with a tight hug and rock him until he relaxed. Then she would sit with him, all day if needed, until she figured out what he needed. Ava never wanted to see her little brother upset and that night, Levi decided to return the favor.

He rubbed the side of her face as her tears flowed. "It's going to be ok, Bug."

"What?" Ava said in a shaky voice. She stared at his mouth like it was some magical portal. Eight years of life and Levi, from what she knew, had never strung together more than two words and now he was saying…

"It's going to be ok." He repeated.

The waterworks that flooded her eyes stopped like the valves were twisted shut. She was shocked, surprised, bewildered, confused, and excited all at the same time. Ava did not know what to say or how to say it even if she somehow came up with the perfect set of words to respond with. She sat up in the bed to see Levi better in the dim light.

He smiled and continued to rub her cheek. His small hand barely covered her jagged scar. It felt warm. The ache and dull pain did not follow his caress. The sweet gesture relaxed her like a hot compress on weary muscles.

What would happen to him? There was that question again. Ava could not shake it. Those few words haunted her thoughts.

A nearby horn honked twice. Ava brushed the thoughts of Levi to the side as the image of Rhea and her new life filled its absence. Her family was now the past and her future was outside in the passenger seat of a slightly used and borrowed, technically stolen, mustard yellow Jeep Wrangler. Rhea was growing impatient, and those two honks would be Ava's only warnings.

If she took much longer, Rhea would either drive off and leave Ava there to find her own way back or she would storm her way into Ava's home and rip apart the ties that bind herself. Ava would have bet a full life's wages on the latter being Rhea's first choice. Breaking those ties was a part of the climb and Ava needed to do it on her own. But Rhea had never been averse to forcing a situation to her liking.

"I knew this was a mistake. I could have left last night while you two were arguing over the property taxes," Ava said.

Her father looked up with surprise.

"Yeah, I heard. I've heard a bucket full over the years." Her eyes narrowed. "But you two have the nerve to question me about Levi." Ava halfway laughed through the whole thing. "And what are you crying for?" Her gaze turned to her mother. "You want me to stick around the Glen and turn out like you, popping out kids? You want me to sit at home, being some glorified housewife, accomplishing nothing? Sorry…" Ava shook her head. Her lips curled as she spoke. "But I'm not sorry," Ava barked. "You can keep your mediocre tentacles latched around Levi, but I will not be held down here any longer."

Ava picked up her suitcase and turned to leave the house. She turned her back on the people who raised her and the home that provided her with shelter. Her father tried one last desperate attempt to control his daughter and steer her down a path that was more traditional and suitable to her parent's liking.

He rushed from his wife's side and restrained Ava by grabbing her wrist. He reached for the suitcase with his other hand. "We are not done talking." He pulled with all his might, but he could not wrench the suitcase from her grip.

Ava turned to him. She glared at him. Her eyes were as cold as an arctic wind in the dead of winter. The way Ava looked down at him with those cold eyes, he could no longer recognize her. The person in front of him was a stranger, cloaked in the skin of his beautiful, chubby-cheeked daughter, Avalee.

Her father screamed in horror. He released his tight grip on her wrist and the luggage. He fell back to the floor. Her father's eyes were as wide as dinner plates. Those frightened eyes looked around every corner of the kitchen. His wife rushed over to his side in an instant. His body trembled like a lone leaf in a strong breeze that was trying its best to hold onto the safety of its mother branch. His eyes locked on to his daughter's face, flabbergasted. A cold sweat dripped from his armpits and down his ribs. Beads of sweat collected at the rim of his forehead like condensation on an ice-cold bottle of beer. His mouth was dry as sandpaper. His palms were clammy.

"Don't ever touch me again," Ava said, as calm as a bathing baby.

Within those few seconds that her father held on tight to Ava's wrist, all his fears and the darkest thoughts from his childhood rushed to the forefront of his mind. They stood there, all of them, as menacing and as dreadful as he remembered, collectively in the kitchen, as real as anything he had ever seen in his life. They all stared at him like a starving connoisseur eyeing an eight-course meal, each paired with its adult beverage.

After that, she was gone. Avalee 'Bug' Wilson left out of her parent's lives for good. A few months later, Ava's mother, Sasha Wilson died in her sleep, a month before her forty-seventh birthday. At her last check-up two years earlier, her primary care physician remarked on how youthful she looked and acted. She had a clean bill of health. Sasha had never been sick in the past six years. Not even a runny nose or persistent cough interrupted her health. Regrettably, the coroner had no answers for her husband of twenty-five magical years.

The news of her mother's sudden death made its way to Ava's ears. The revelation seemed to open old wounds that Ava did not realize she still had. The pain was sharp but quick. Like most things around that time, the heartache lasted for mere moments and then Ava's mind and heart settled back to its normal rhythm. By the time her father, Chuck 'CT' Wilson, died two years later, the unfortunate news did not cause a second thought.

Ava heard about her father's death through the same channels as before. She spent a moment processing it, about five minutes, and then she was onto something else. Ava had been changed by her climb. Death was nothing more than a means to a desirable end that, in the end, ultimately meant nothing.

Ava often wondered why Followers of the Abyss, such as Rhea or even her Den Mother, Betta, would tell her about the passing of her family members. Was it some sort of test? Maybe they wanted to see if her ties were truly broken or if her resolve and dedication to the climb would be weakened by a personal loss. Ava did not know, and she decided not to ask any questions. The people she could have asked would probably not have given her the answers anyway. It was like most things in her new life; she would know when she was ready to know, and at that particular time, Ava must not have been ready and that was okay with her.

After both of her parent's deaths, her now 12-year-old brother Levi was shipped off to live with their second cousins, the Bookers, in Kingsport, Tennessee. Ava had only met the Bookers three times in her life. Each time their cousins came to visit them in Red Glen, they were on their way to some other destination. Visiting national parks was a big thing for their family. Every summer they would stuff themselves into their wood panel station wagon and head out on a two-week adventure of camping, hiking, and sightseeing.

Ava's parents did not like to travel too far from home. "Everything we need is in Montana and in Red Glen," her father would say. Both of them were born in the heart of Montana and neither one had any urge to move elsewhere. It was a quality that they did not share with their firstborn.

Sometimes, when the nights were quiet or the days were rather uneventful and Ava let her mind drift, she could almost feel Levi out there, somewhere. When that sensation was at its strongest, it felt like they were in the same room, once again, staring up at the glow-in-the-dark stickers that dotted his bedroom ceiling. She would talk to him about her day and the things she learned in class and Levi, still mute at the time, would respond with a grunt or two every few minutes. She took it as his way of saying "Uh huh," "Oh," or "That's fascinating."

If anything could pull her back to the past and her old connections, even after all of the climbing she had done so far, it would have been the memories of little Levi. She was attached to him with an invisible string wrapped tightly around her core, mentally and physically, since the day he was born. Only after Ava's final test and the Traveler's eight-pointed star being branded on her wrist, did those feelings fade away.

The revelation of that missing thread would not happen until after her little brothers' fate was already sealed. His death was never mentioned. Ava received no word about her brother from anyone that might have known of him. A trip through the Abyss's rings of all places was where his demise was discovered.

Ava had risen high enough through the ranks as a Traveler to gain access to the very bottom levels of hell. She spent years traversing its seven main rings. She watched as the massive gust of wind battered half-naked and malnourished bodies with hurricane forces, slamming them against jagged rocks. Ava had strolled through icy rains that fell like jagged frozen daggers, impaling the unfortunate who ran for shelter that they would never find. She crossed the river Styx, past the wild-eyed lunatics that attacked anyone near them and over the bodies trapped under the cursed river's waters in a perpetual state of drowning. She passed by the flaming coffins and listened to the inhabitants' tortured screams like a psychopath's music playlist. She traveled through the seemingly endless scorched desert and saw the terror in the eyes of the damned that had to walk through its burning sands for an eternity. At times, throughout her travels, Ava would join in and take part in some of the torture that ran rampant on the different rings. Ava grew accustomed to all of the horrors and began to enjoy dishing out pain to others while using various objects and spells given to her by that level's Lord.

At the very bottom, the last ring before the throne room, Ava saw him there. She stopped sixty yards away. Her little brother Levi was encased in ice up to his scrawny neck, shivering in the depths. Frost covered his face, biting at his exposed skin. His lips were a pale blue. His ears were blackened at the tips. Thankfully his eyes were sealed shut. Ava did not want him to see her down there walking around freely. She would never want him to know that she was a part of anything like that.

Ava looked away. Her mind became a storm. A chill passed through her body, the likes of which she had never felt in her life. A guttural scream almost leapt from her mouth. She clenched her jaw tight as a vise. Ava wanted him to hear her voice, but she knew that would be a mistake. Her heart ached before exploding into a thousand pieces. The shards from her heart were flung outwards like bits of shrapnel, stabbing all her vital organs. On the inside, she bawled like a child as she walked away. Ava sobbed for her baby brother like a child whose favorite blankie had been taken away. On the outside, she was emotionless. A thousand-yard stare decorated her face like a war-torn army vet.

Ava's body went into autopilot as she passed by a few Travelers and harvester Demons. Not a single hint of what was bubbling beneath made it to the surface. She looked around to see if any of the numerous demons or Travelers had noticed a slight change in her demeanor. The rings of the Abyss were not the place for outbursts or snap judgments. They walked around the rest of the human popsicles, talking amongst themselves. Some skipped through the hundreds of exposed heads like a field of daisies, randomly kicking a few heads as they passed by.

Ava had to keep her emotions under control until she returned to the Earth's plane. Even then, she would need to wait until she was completely solitaire before she could let out her feelings. An outburst or any hysterical action could be seen as something to be dealt with and there would be plenty who would not mind being assigned to the task.

"There's no sense in complaining about the buzzing if you're going to sit still in the hornet's nest." Ava's mother would often say that to her husband whenever he would complain about his micromanaging supervisor, Colin Shipley. Every other week for an entire year, her father would threaten to punch Colin right in the mouth. "I swear if he says one more thing to me, Sasha. One more thing… I'm going to knock his teeth out." She knew he would never do it, but he would come into the house, fuming about his workday and Colin, and then like clockwork, he would say something about giving him a knuckle sandwich. She would calm him down and tell him how he should quit and find something better, but he would not do it. Her father would explain how the crew needed him and how he was the only one who had enough experience. And every time, her mother said the same thing, "there's no sense in complaining about the buzzing if you're going to sit still in the hornet's nest."

Erik McGowan

-15-
WRATH

Ava's eyes fluttered open. Her brain throbbed. It squeezed against the inside of her skull. It felt like her brain was trying to make an escape from its confines. *I'm so tired.* Her body glistened. Sweat soaked her shirt. Gluttony, the soul that took her earlier wounds for itself and simultaneously fed her with fuel she needed to keep fighting, had finally run out. Her bones ached. Her muscles begged for another moment of much-needed rest and recovery. Her stomach growled for more sustenance. Ava was all out of fuel and was barely running on fumes. The demons that had been watching her knew it.

The shadows that were cast about the room crept toward her like a colony of stalking cats. Inch by inch, they crawled over the brittle wood floorboards towards her limp body. Ava watched as the darkness moved forward, unable to move more than a few inches to escape. Fatigue held tight to her body, holding her down in place.

Once those demons got a hold of her, Ava's eternal punishment would start. At first, there would be some light forms of torture like ripping off her fingernails one at a time to prime her nervous system for things to come. All of the Demons, Travelers, Hellions, and Lords on each Ring of the Abyss would get their turn with her next. They would tear at her flesh, dismember her appendages, or crush a bone or two until Ava was nothing more than a bloody lump of meat. After that, her destroyed body would be restored and her cursed soul would be dragged through to the next level of Hell where she would get tortured again and again. She would spend several decades on each level, until after a couple of centuries, Ava would finally arrive at the 8th level and be placed in front of her sweet little brother, tied to a stake with her eyelids peeled off so she could never close them. Upon that stake, Ava would be forced to watch as her little brother received the same agony as she had. For the rest of eternity, they would force her to watch. That would be her payment for betrayal.

Thoughts of that inevitability played through her head in a continuous loop as she stared into the increasing blackness that surrounded her. She knew what was there, hiding in those shadows. If a person knew where to look and they focused on the slightest of movements, they could be seen by anyone. The Capatus Furem, Shadow Demons, lurked and squirmed through the darkness.

Charcoal hands reached out from the shadows. Fingers, long and almost impossibly thin, wiggled with excitement as they approached her stagnant limbs.

Ava's body trembled as they approached. She was too tired to do much else. The one remaining light source that dangled in the middle of the room dimmed a little, allowing the Capatus Furem to spread further. Whispers crept out from the darkness. Voices strained and deep, called out to Ava in a low hiss. Their voices sounded as if their mouths were right next to her ear, almost touching her earlobe. She tried to muffle the voices with hand earmuffs, but the sound was the same. She heard their saliva, if they even had that, smacking in their mouths. She could feel the heat from their breath as if they were crowded around her in a tight circle.

They converged on her as the room grew darker, but they did not go too far. The incandescent bulb was enough to stave off even the boldest Shadow Demon. They shrieked as their shadowy figures made their way to the cable hanging from the ceiling.

Ava looked up to watch their progress. The light swung as a few of the Capatus Furem's claws fumbled at its cable. The rest crouched on the ground or clung to the walls like ancient stone gargoyles, continuing their vicious taunts. The light flickered again, drawing the demons closer for a brief second before moving back from the oncoming light like a tidal wave.

A low voice broke into the middle of their chatter, as low as a shout from three acres away. The Capatus Furem continued their verbal torment—but the voice in her head grew louder by the second, dominating her ears and thoughts.

"Concentrate Ava," the voice repeated. Each time the words were spoken they grew in intensity. "Concentrate."

The voice, now as clear as her inner thoughts, silenced the others.

The last light went out as the filament burned up, fading into the darkness that had already swallowed the rest of the room. Sounds of scurrying feet and fumbling hands echoed off the metal walls.

"Be brave." Ava could hear her father say. "Be brave, little Bug. If only for one night." Ava closed her eyes and finally gave in.

It's time.

The tattooed bands around her brown arms flashed with a blue-white light that partially flooded the room and exposed the Capatus Furem who stood in front of her with its intensity. They shielded the pits on their inky faces from the light that radiated from her skin.

The demons were almost as black as the shadows they lived in. They were as skinny as broomsticks and half of Ava's height. Their arms were long enough to scrape the ground while they stood at their full height. Several of the demons hung from the ceiling by their large hands or feet, half of their bodies still in their jet-black shadowy homes. The closest demons, who were merely inches away, melted into nothingness from the blue-white light within seconds of being exposed to it.

The tattooed armbands spun on Ava's skin in opposite directions. Ava's eyes jerked open, wide as a manhole cover. They glowed with the same blue-white light as the tattoos. From her gaped mouth, wispy white smoke puffed out like a steam train with each breath. Ava gave a low growl with each exhale.

The remaining hundreds of Capatus Furem stood still and silent in her presence, frozen in her glow. Ava attacked without warning. Her speed was beyond anything she could have mustered with her previous spells and incantations. She tore through them with her bare hands. Her hands were like heavy bear claws, ripping, slashing, and smacking each of the demons that were within range. She tore them from the ceiling and walls. She ripped off their limbs and bit through a few necks and faces. The injured Capatus Furem screamed from the pain.

She obliterated every demon she got her hands on within seconds. Hundreds of them had packed the small office by the time they managed to turn off the last remaining light, but now, after two minutes of her relentless and savage attacks, less than fifty remained.

A few tried to retreat to the Abyss through the shadows from which they sprang but they were easily stopped before they could fully escape. Ava yanked them out of their shadowy refuge and then destroyed their inky bodies for good by crushing them or ripping them in half at the waist.

Her movements were fast and loose, precise and terrifying. Ava had become a beast, possessed by wrath, with only destruction and violence on her mind.

After finishing off the last remnants of the Capatus Furem, Ava turned her focus on her enclosure. She attacked the metal door with the same ferocity that destroyed all of the demons in the room. Her bare hands slammed into the metal door with an unyielding force. The door shook from the impact. It cried out with loud clanks as it tried to endure the beating.

The metal cage was no match for her increased power. Ava knocked the metal door off its hinges, sending it flying out into the factory. The nearby birds that made their homes in the surrounding trees for the night, took flight from the sudden commotion that was occurring in the previously abandoned derelict building.

The mass exodus of the terrified flock blotted out a quarter of the moon's light for almost a full minute.

-16-
COMING DAWN

Rhea leaned over the railing and looked down at the unconscious Greys sprawled on the ground. She looked over their bruised bodies. Betta paced in the background, visibly upset, talking to Rhea, but Rhea did not take the time to listen. Whatever Betta was saying could have been important, something crucial to their efforts, but Rhea could not be reached. Even though she was staring down at the remnants of the chaos that happened below, Rhea's mind and ears were tuned to the office where Ava was trapped. She listened intently, trying to hear any sound that would give her the outcome of Ava's predicament.

From where Rhea stood, the old shabby office seemed relatively quiet for the first thirty minutes. Then she could hear some wrestling and possible footsteps, but it was all non-discernible.

There were two loud bangs. Betta stopped talking. Rhea spun around just in time to see the metal door that had trapped Ava inside with the Capatus Furem flying in her direction. Luckily for Rhea, her reaction time was just enough to avoid the same incident that laid her out, unconscious at the tavern. She dove out of the way, landing inches away from the speeding door. Her body ached from the impact of the unforgiving metal catwalk.

The door collided with the railing where Rhea had been standing. The sturdy guard rail split from the impact. The metal creaked and the platform shook with the force of a small earthquake. The door was launched off the catwalk, spinning like a thrown axe, down to the factory floor below. It bounced off a few of the milling stations like a pinball and then came to rest on the leg of an unconscious Grey. The pain from his lower leg being shattered by the metal door snapped him awake with the potency of a fistful of smelling salts. He cried out in disbelief. He kicked at the metal mass, trying his best to pry the door off with his other foot. His screams and curses were thunderous but not loud enough to arouse any of his unconscious brethren.

Rhea lay where she landed. Her eyes were as wide as the office's empty door frame. She peered into the dark room trying to catch any movement as she took her time climbing to her feet.

Battle-hardened Betta was unfazed by the flying door. "She escaped the Capatus Furem," Betta spat.

Betta stepped towards the unknown that cloaked itself in the room's shadows. Rhea reflexively grabbed Betta's shoulder. Normally, Rhea would not dare interrupt Betta in the middle of a confrontation or even touch her in a controlling manner, but in this dire moment, she was compelled. There was something in that room and it was dangerous. Rhea could feel the danger in her bones.

Betta looked down at Rhea's hand with a grimace. "Remove your hand. Now."

Rhea let go without a single word of defiance and stepped to the side. The sound of deep, heavy breathing crept through the doorless frame, followed by a blur of blue and brown. A savage Ava vaulted from the darkness. Light spilled from her tattooed bands like glow rods. Rhea shrieked from the sight, stumbling backward. The ever-prepared Betta hopped to the side, away from Ava's attack. Ava landed on the metal catwalk, in a crouch. The metal warped around her feet with her arm plunged elbow-deep into the catwalk floor.

Ava's skin looked thin and very vascular. Veins and arteries crowded Ava's flesh like a bundle of cables. Muscles bulged and blood vessels pulsated as she breathed. The tattooed bands around her arms revolved at the speed of a jumbo jet turbine, projecting that intense blue-white light.

As quickly as she landed, Ava sprung after Betta. Her great claw-like hands extended out, swiping at Betta's small frame. Betta stood her ground, waiting for the split second before Ava's hand would reach her body to counterattack.

Betta knew that Ava would rush in. It was a habit Ava had that she seemed to never get rid of. Open-palmed, Betta thrust her hand at Ava's throat. Her sleeve made an audible pop from the force. The perfectly timed attack, which had been practiced and honed over several decades missed after Ava's quick sidestepped.

Ava swiped at her again. Betta sunk to the ground in an instant. She watched as Ava's upper body drifted overhead. She aimed and struck at both of Ava's kidneys. It was a pincer strike. Her arms came in from both sides like a mighty ant's jaws.

Betta was so focused, so sure of her physical rebuttal, that she did not notice Ava's knee until it was too late. Ava's knee smashed into Betta's face, launching her head like a soccer ball. Betta's body trailed behind, following its arc. Rhea watched as Ava chased down Betta's limp body.

Betta tried to climb to her feet, but Ava was constantly attacking. None of her counters were working. She tried to strike at her legs to slow Ava down or to topple her, but Ava leapt over the top. Betta tried to catch her on her blind side with a counterattack, but that too missed.

Betta could see it in her eyes, Ava was not calculating her movements or strategizing her attacks. She was moving way too fast for anything like that. It was all instinct and primal rage. As soon as Betta started an attack, Ava would already be in the process of striking again. All of Ava's movements were focused on attack. After a couple of minutes, it became abundantly clear that Betta could do nothing but dodge. She had been successfully evading each strike, but each miss was a close graze. Tiny cuts that were as thin as paper cuts appeared on her exposed skin. Betta was being pushed to her limits.

Ava responded with a roundhouse kick to Betta's ribs. Betta took the full brunt of the kick and crashed into the wall of the office with a grunt. She bounced off the wall like a ping-pong ball and stumbled forward. Betta rolled to avoid the next blow. Ava's hand broke through the concrete facade like a thin wood plank. Chunks of the concrete cascaded from the wall and fell through the holes of the catwalk.

Betta looked up from her roll to see Ava's foot inches from her face. She had enough time to protect her face by dodging but not enough time to avoid it completely. The front kick slammed into Betta's shoulder. She fell backward with a quick jerk. Betta hollered, pulling her hand up to her face. Three of her fingers; the middle, ring, and pinky were either broken or dislocated.

When Betta finished her initial roll to avoid Ava's punch, her fingers slipped into some of the holes in the grated floor. Betta did not notice until she felt the snap. She cradled her ragged hand with the opposite. Betta tried again to climb to her feet while cradling her hand, but Ava was relentless with her assault.

Betta cried out to the immobilized Rhea who stood near the railing that was contorted by the metal door. Her words fell on deaf ears. Rhea's hands trembled, vibrating the railing she held tight. Her eyes were wide and erratic as she watched a savage Ava punch and kick after Betta. The force of Ava's blows destroyed whatever they hit with relative ease.

Betta tried to get Rhea's attention one last time. "Rhea," she shouted as she continued to evade. Her damaged hand was held tight to her chest. "She's possessed. I need your help."

Betta was right. Ava was stuck in a possession loop. Rhea could see it with her own eyes. She could smell the wrath spewing from Ava's pores like overused cheap cologne. And Ava, even in her mindless state, could smell the fear oozing from Rhea.

A possession loop is a rare occurrence in the Abyss. Depending on the sin, the possessed can become trapped in what is essentially a feedback loop. The sin is committed by the possessed, and the possessor responds by committing acts on their Ring, giving the possessed more power to use and the loop continues. When this occurs, the possessed is usually 'put down' before the loop has a chance to cycle through more than two dozen times. Ava and Wrath had reached that mark well before escaping the confines of the office.

The bridge between the possessor and the possessed can be broken on either end. Betta, Rhea, or any other who might know of the current situation could stop the soul in the Abyss to end the loop. But because of the ward that Ava had placed around the building, Betta and Rhea were unable to open a Gate to escape the factory to the Abyss. That reality left Betta and Rhea with the harder choice of the two, overpowering the possessed Ava here and now with everything they could muster.

Rhea closed her eyes and shook her head. Her mouth quivered. In that split second when Betta was shocked by Rhea's reaction, Ava struck her in the stomach. The force from the blow lifted Betta off her feet and into the air several inches.

Betta crashed down from the punch, landing on her knees. Her face twisted up with equal parts pain and confusion. The Fighting Fish gasped for air as if she had been pulled from the comfort of the sea and outstretched on dry land. She tried to stand but was unable to get up from her hands and knees. She retched several times before all the contents of her gut evacuated in a quick and violent burst. Bile and half-digested oatmeal spilled on the catwalk, dripping through the grates, and splashed on the ground below, creating a bizarre and violent inkblot. Betta's eyes bulged. Her face flushed with a deep red. She tried her best to regain her breathing, but it did not work. Betta tried to stand up again, but every one of her muscles felt weak as if she had been using them nonstop for weeks. She could do nothing but roll over to her side. Betta stared at Rhea before her eyes glazed over and then closed.

Ava pivoted on her heels and launched herself at Rhea.

"No," Rhea shrieked, as she clamored away.

Ava's glowing eyes watched her. Smoke drifted out of her open jaws. She grew closer. Her hands flexed like a defensive crab's claws.

"Don't do this," Rhea shouted. "I was following orders."

Ava continued her march forward. The metal clanked with each step.

"Please, Ava." Rhea stuck out a hand, reaching for Ava's face.

Ava crouched down to get closer. She drew her hand back for a powerful slash.

Rhea leaned forward. Her soft hand grazed Ava's face, stopping her in mid-stride. "Please, talk to me," she said.

The moonlit factory grew just a little bit brighter as the darkness of wrath withdrew. Ava's breathing slowed. Her wrath was partially pacified. The possession loop seemed to be broken or at the very least, slowed.

"I didn't want to fight. I don't want to fight." Rhea bushed her hand across Ava's cheek again. "I only came for the souls you took. Remember?" Rhea tried to reason with Ava. "I was your initiate. We spent years together. I wouldn't try to hurt you. We have a connection." She pulled on her shirt, exposing the ink dot that was just above her left collarbone.

Ava's consciousness clawed itself back to the foreground. Her posture straightened. Her glowing eyes reverted to her natural dark brown. The grimace that contorted her face relaxed as well as the muscles in the rest of her body. The bands of wrath that encircled her arms dimmed and slowed in their revolutions. Ava's mind had made a return. She rubbed at the tiny dot on her skin.

"You're back," Rhea said, seeing the changes that had occurred. She wiped a few specks of blood off the side of Ava's face. Rhea stood.

The dull colors of the factory grew more saturated as Rhea talked. Birds that previously scattered from the office door being knocked off its hinges, could be heard faintly chirping in the distance, as if morning were soon to follow. The cry from the injured Grey continued like a morning alarm.

Rhea looked around at the carnage that Ava had created. The bodies sprawled on the floor of the factory floor below them, the dented metal door that now took up residence with the unused machines, the ransacked display office with its shattered plexiglass, dented metal wall, the scattered props, and Betta, curled up on the catwalk like a weeping child, unconscious and drooling. She touched Ava again, this time lightly on the hand. "We can fix this." Her voice was smooth. Rhea moved closer. "I can tell them you made your escape after you defeated Betta." Rhea took another step as her hand slid up to Ava's elbow.

With every light touch and with every soft-spoken word, Ava relaxed. Her breathing slowed. She nodded as she listened to Rhea spin her silk.

"Don't worry about the Greys," she tapped Ava's elbow, "They knew what they signed up for. Well, most of them." Rhea smiled. Her eyes twinkled like the brightest star on the blackest of nights. Her skin almost seemed like it glowed from the sheen of sweat that coated her forehead. "We can work this out." Rhea stepped closer. She was now less than a foot away. "You can go back on the run and… I can pretend to chase you."

Rhea's skin felt soft as her hand brushed up against Ava's arm, making its way up to her shoulder. Rhea looked over Ava's tattoos as she did. The blue-white light that was projecting through her armbands dimmed to being barely visible.

Ava studied Rhea's face. Her breathing steadied to a meditative rhythm. All her senses reverted from their previously heightened state. She could feel the soft, familiarity of Rhea's skin. How long had it been since she touched her? Rhea's scent wafted into Ava's nose. How long has it been since she smelled her? In an instant, Ava's mind shot back to their early days, the secrets they shared, the locations they traveled to.

"You look exhausted," Rhea said. "Why don't you sit down."

Rhea was completely right. Ava was exhausted. Her eyelids were heavy. She felt dehydrated. Ava could feel the sweat dripping down her face. *For a couple of minutes.* She lowered herself to the metal grating. It felt good to finally sit and take a break, even though the metal jabbed at her butt and thighs like Lego blocks. Ava had been practically running around for hours on end. She wanted and needed this break without being knocked unconscious first.

"That's it. Relax. It's ok." Rhea sat down with Ava like a gossiping teen, ready to hear all the secrets from her best friend. She continued to rub Ava's arm. The tattooed bands slowed to a crawl before reverting to their original onyx pigment. Rhea looked over Ava's body, her arms, the skin that peeked through the tears in her jeans, and her palms. "Is this what you did with those souls?"

"Yes," Ava said. Her eyelids drifted to half-mast. "I took a little piece from each. It would have been impossible to remove the whole thing." Her words drifted out of her mouth like a falling feather.

"One from each level…" Rhea turned over Ava's hands, seeing the envy and greed tattoos for the first time.

Ava nodded, smiling like a tired drunk.

"Is that—" Rhea tucked her lip. Her face flushed with color. "Is that how you did all of this?"

Ava nodded again. Her eyes were drawn to Rhea's wet lips.

"Wow." Rhea smiled, touching her leg. "You are so strong. You're like Nathan."

Ava's heart fluttered from the compliment. She opened her mouth to speak.

Rhea continued. "No wonder you could evade us for so long." She played with Ava's hands, interlocking their fingers. "This time, I'm going to go with you."

Ava shook her head, protesting the idea.

"No. I'm going to do it. We can run together. You and me. Going wherever we want, whenever we want. I don't need any of this."

Ava stared into her blue eyes as she spoke. A smile snuck its way onto her face.

"You know I've missed you, right?" Rhea pulled Ava's hand to her chest, right above her heart. "It's true. I know I can be jealous at times, but I've never meant to hurt your feelings. Do you know what I've been doing since you left me? Trying to replace you. All those Greys… One day I woke up and I was the leader of a cult." She laughed. "Even Kizzy." Rhea paused for a moment. "I wish you never left. But now, we can be together again. Tearing up the towns." Rhea laughed.

Ava looked away. A frown replaced her smile. She wanted the same thing, to be lost again in the good times like before. But you can never really go back. The past will always be the past. *But the future. We could make the future better.*

"Or not. It's up to you. Come on. Let's get out of here." Rhea stood, pulling Ava along with her. "Once you take down the ward, we can step out into the fresh air and come up with a plan."

They both walked towards the stairs leading down to the factory floor.

-17-
FRAUD

"By the way," Rhea said, walking behind Ava, slightly to her right. "Do you have any more of that ink left? I wouldn't mind getting some tattoos too. A few like you or Kizzy."

Ava looked down at Betta's body as they passed her. *Clean.* Betta lay like a cooked shrimp, unconscious, with a sly grin on her face. She looked as if she was having the greatest dream of her life. The kind of dream that would turn you fierce if you were to be awakened before its conclusion.

"Yeah," Ava said. "I have plenty left." Ava cocked her leg and kicked backward like a startled horse. The heel of her foot hit Rhea in the chest. The forceful kick knocked Rhea off her feet and sent her tumbling for two yards. A small crude blade, as jagged as a piece of cracked glass clattered on the catwalk where Rhea once stood. Ava was on top of Rhea as soon as she stopped rolling. Her foot pressed against Rhea's chest, pinning her down. "Charms." She glared at Rhea. Ava's muscles tightened as her lips peeled back from her teeth like a growling wolf. "You used those rings. You had me," Ava nodded, "You had me good, but your influence affected Betta too."

Rhea looked over at Betta's body. Ava was right. Betta's defenses against the charms were nonexistent since she was unconscious. Rhea shook her head. "No," she said, her voice quivering.

"No more lies Rhea Kane," Ava spat. "Dismoveo cupido." Ava swept her hand in front of Rhea, inches from her face. Her fingers latched onto the invisible cloak that shrouded Rhea's body. Ava ripped back the veil like plastic wrap. It stretched at first, distorting everything around Rhea like a carnival's funhouse mirror, then it ripped and peeled away, exposing the truth that Rhea had been hiding for decades. Within an instant, the bright, colorful, abandoned factory turned back to its lifeless, dull, and bland self.

"Why?" Rhea cried. "Why did you do that?" She tried her best to cover her face with her arms. Rhea's self-imposed veil of lust had finally been stripped away. Rhea's true image was exposed. Her wrinkled face snuck glances from behind her frail arms.

Rhea was old. She was much older than Ava would have ever thought. A guess of the mid-nineties would have been a compliment. Rhea's skin was either wrinkled, hanging loose, thin as rice paper, spotted with psoriasis, or a combination of them all. Everything but her eyes showed Rhea's age. Rhea's eyes looked as blue and as sharp as they were when they first met all those years ago.

"Why are you doing this?" Rhea scooted back to the rail at the edge of the catwalk. "Why? Why didn't you run? Why didn't you run like you always do?"

Ava approached her without talking.

Rhea wrapped her arms around the rail, tight as a scared child with a teddy bear. She balled up in fear, turning her face from her former recruit.

"Why didn't I run?" Ava shouted. "You know exactly why. You and me—we were looking for something in the Abyss. Both of us. You never found your prize—because you stopped looking… but not me," Ava said. She grabbed Rhea's shoulder. "I stumbled into it— blindly, without even knowing it. I found what I was looking for at the very bottom of the Abyss, neck deep in a block of ice. My little brother was buried there. Terrified and lonely." Ava's eyes cooled to an ice blue. Her lips pulled back as she spoke, exposing more of her teeth and gums. The tattooed bands on her arms began spinning.

"They took his innocent soul." Ava's grip tightened on Rhea's brittle shoulder.

Rhea screamed in agony. No matter the amount of pain she felt, Rhea refused to come out of hiding.

"And when I came to you," Ava continued, "my Initiate— my friend, you…" Blood trickled from where Ava's short nails pierced Rhea's shoulder.

***

Ava wanted answers. Every ounce of her being needed answers, but she also needed to choose who she should ask and how she would formulate the question. For the next three days, Ava spent her spare time thinking through her options like a Go match, trying to figure out every move and every possible counter. On one end, she concluded, that no matter how she went about it, at the very least, they would be watching her from here on out. Everything she does from now on has to be deliberate and calculated. Asking anyone directly with enough power to know the exact circumstances of her brother's soul would be a death wish.

A simple talk amongst 'colleagues' and she could gather enough information to fill in the rest of the blanks on her own. She would have to piece it together from several different conversations to avoid exposing her motives but the time in getting those stories would be a small price. Rhea Kane was an automatic mark for the first step of her espionage. She was the closest thing Ava had to a friend in the Abyss. To test their bonds, Ava would bear a part of her soul that had been sheltered for some time now. She would open up just enough to read Rhea's position on the matter and then seal herself shut once more.

During a late evening after a few hours of slow drinking, Ava made her move.

"How many rings... have you traveled?" Ava probed.

Their individual exploration of the Abyss was a topic they never really discussed. The two never traveled to the Rings of the Abyss together or happened to spot each other passing by like some plain Jane seeing an old classmate on the street of their small town. Ava knew that Rhea had to have been at least once. Though Rhea was not branded like Ava to allow her extended stays and deeper climbs, the unique smell of the Rings and its essence lingered about Rhea like any other who had stepped foot into its realm.

Rhea sipped her beer, not making eye contact. Her eyes surveyed the expansive valley. The sun tiptoed near the horizon. The treetops gently swayed in the wind. "Three."

Only three? Is she lying? Ava pondered the thought, but she could not decide. It is true that Travelers spend more time traversing the Rings than the average Initiate, but everyone had at least one person they would search for. *There is no way...*

Rhea turned to look at Ava with glassy eyes. The beer bottle hovered close to her lips.

"I was wondering," Ava added, "throughout your travels, have you ever seen your mother?"

From what Rhea told Ava about her mother, it was a foregone conclusion that she would end up somewhere down there in the realm of the Abyss. Her mother did not have a decent bone in her body. Rhea never divulged everything her mother had done to her, but the physical abuse was one of the tamer acts that she had to endure.

Rhea gulped down the last bit of the beer and tossed the empty green bottle over the cliff. Ava watched as it dropped into the nearby canopy, ruffling the leaves, and then disappearing into the rest of its foliage. Rhea grabbed another bottle from her bag and wrenched the cap off with her teeth. She took another swig, swishing it around her mouth while she seemingly thought over the question. An audible "ahhh" left her mouth after she swallowed. "Not once. And I've been searching."

I've been searching. So, it was more than just three times. Ava took her time, nursing her bottle, analyzing every word and inflection. Rhea was extremely blarney when she wanted to be. Which in turn made her almost perfectly cast as an Initiate. It also made it tremendously hard to read between her lines or judge the sincerity of her words.

"I thought I saw Mama once," Rhea continued, "on the first level." She paused to hiccup. "She was hiding in the mountains like most of them do. That woman was fresh-out-the-womb naked, trembling from the chill of the hard winds." She turned towards Ava. Her eyes were full of hate. "Something about her…" Rhea looked around in search of the right word or words, but they eluded her tipsy brain. "Maybe it was her stringy, matted red hair or her freckled, pasty back." Rhea's face coalesced into a grimace. "I charged at her, yelling her name." Her face softened. "I'm sure you've noticed by now how the elements don't affect

Travelers, or whoever has the star." Rhea pulled her necklace out from under her shirt. The Traveler's star shook from the thin golden chain.

Ava looked down at her Traveler's star, branded on the inside of her left wrist. She rubbed over it with her thumb as she nodded. The act was soothing. The brand burned on occasion, even if she had not traveled through a Gate in some time. It was almost like a reminder of her pact with the Abyss and everything that entailed.

"Well, she couldn't hear me over the howling wind," Rhea said, scratching at her eyebrow with her thumb. The beer sloshed around from the movement. "And I didn't notice at the time. I was as mad as a box of frogs."

Every once in a while, Ava noticed, Rhea would say something that would catch her off guard. Ava believed it was the truth, coming out for a quick peek. Her real self was on display for that split second. The self that they all hid from each other was like a secret treasure. "Expose everything but yourself." A lesson taught to her by Betta, the Fighting Fish. "Knowledge is power and the powerful wield knowledge with the skills of a surgeon."

"I grabbed her by the back of the head," Rhea mimicked the motion, demonstrating it on herself. "Getting a full grip of her dirty hair, I slung her gaunt body off the side of the cliff. She flew like a plucked bird." Rhea said. She smiled as she thought back to that moment.

Ava was neither shocked by the act of violence nor the foregone conclusion of mistaken identity. She had long since been immune to such stories or acts. As a Traveler, she saw plenty of heinous acts on a daily basis. To her, the story was just another day, an average Monday.

"I caught a glimpse of the woman's face right before she bounced off the first jagged rock." She sighed. "When I saw that it wasn't her, I was as disappointed as a plump goose in a pillow factory."

The south? Which region? Over the years, Ava has heard hundreds of dialects and regional slang, but her mind never sorted them by their region. It kept what was needed and nothing else. Ava did need to understand dialects but only to the point of being able to answer with the correct response. Its etymology did not matter to her in the slightest. But right now, she was wishing it had.

Rhea giggled and then hiccuped. She covered her mouth with the back of her hand. "But I still like to hold on to that memory. It always brings a smile to my face." Rhea smiled again. Deep pits formed in her cheeks. "Did you see yours?"

"Mine?" The question caught Ava off guard. Her mind had been stuck elsewhere at that moment.

"Your family. Mother, father?"

"No." Ava flicked her empty bottle off the side of the cliff. It flipped end over end as it dropped, clanging off the side of the cliff. "I've traveled each Ring, over and over. I haven't seen either one of them yet."

If Only For One Night

"All of them?" Rhea looked at Ava with surprise.

What was that? Ava nodded. "Yeah… All the way to the bottom." Ava looked back out to the wilderness. The sky was a clear deep blueberry blue, spreading itself out for miles. A few mountains in the distance poked through the expansive horizon like rocky islands in a sea of trees and multicolored leaves.

"What would you do if you saw them?" Rhea took another big gulp.

Ava opened her mouth to speak with the confidence that she had regained over the years, but she honestly did not know. She had never thought about it past seeing them on one of the Rings. Every person from her past life made her angry. She wanted to see her past burn, repeatedly. But now, the thought of seeing her parents down there on one of the Rings did not sit well with her. Ava still hated them, but she did not want to see them tortured. She also was not sure anymore. Even if she did have a clear-cut answer, Ava did not know if it was a good idea to tell Rhea anything.

Levi. The name rang through her head like a church bell signaling morning mass. Did she really hate them? Ava was not sure anymore. She had not been sure about many things recently. Seeing Levi stuck in the ice pulled most of her feelings and beliefs into question.

"Ava," Rhea said.

Ava snapped back to the present. With a knee-jerk reaction, the topic that she had been pondering over leapt from her mouth. "I saw my brother. Levi." *Too soon.* Ava was still not quite sure if Rhea would help her or throw her to the wolves. But she could not take back her words. The choice had been made. She hoped her original judgment was the correct one.

Rhea reached over with a delicate hand and touched Ava's bare shoulder. The light touch and the warmth of Rhea's hand loosened Ava's coiled shoulder muscles. "I'm sorry to hear that."

Ava gave a polite smile. She was initially touched by the words and gestures. Then Rhea's words repeated several times in her head, rippling through her thoughts. "I'm sorry to hear that or I'm sorry for your loss," is a perfectly normal response to the death of someone important in a person's life but there were two differences in that situation. Levi did not die. Ava knew that wholeheartedly. He had been taken or he would not be buried in ice at the bottom Ring. And two, Rhea Kane was the one giving the condolences.

Rhea was an Initiate; they did not speak that way unless there was something to gain. Even the shoulder touch was fake. Ava could make out the fraud without looking. It is possible Rhea did not know about her brother's residency since she had never traveled that far, but either way, her actions showed that she did not care.

Ava should have known. They are not really friends, only acquaintances. Her awakening to the truth had been a slow process, but she was fully awake now. From the very beginning, they had been using each other for a better foothold to climb lower into the Abyss.

"You're sorry to hear that?" Ava said. She jerked away from Rhea's hand.

Rhea retracted her hand. "What's wrong?"

A diversion. And just like that, her doubts were gone. Rhea knew something. They all probably knew. Why did they not tell her? Why would they take him? Her parents were free, but they took her sweet little brother. He never did anything to anybody. If there is a such thing as innocence, he was it. But her parents were free of punishment?

Those thoughts ran through her in a split second. She grew more frustrated with every passing moment. Ava was no longer in control of her emotions. If they were watching her, testing her, to see how she would react, well the jig was up.

Ava needed to calm down, but she could not deal with her thoughts about Rhea in front of her face. Escape was Ava's first thought, and she did exactly that. Ava opened a Gate, inches below the cliff face and jumped in, leaving behind Rhea and that horrible conversation.

The treetops juddered from the collapsed portal. Black dust sprinkled down like powdered flour from a dredger, dusting their leaves.

***

Ava relaxed, as she let out a strong exhale. "I had a problem," she nodded, "so I searched some more. I searched for a solution, forgoing every distraction that could stop my goal. I climbed deep into the

Abyss. I walked every ring. I searched each one of them, inch by bloody inch until I got what I needed. One piece of the puzzle from each level." Ava smiled. It was a crooked smile, an all-knowing smile. It was a smile that said that she had an ace up her sleeve, and she had every intention of using it. "I had to do a lot of convincing to get each piece. A whole lot of convincing. Well," Ava smirked, "except for one. I found her—wandering through the ring of Lust, just like you thought."

"Momma...?" Rhea mumbled behind her shield of thin clothes and frail appendages.

"She didn't need any convincing at all. I just mentioned your name and—"

Rhea spun around to see Ava's face. Ava caught her head with both hands, holding Rhea's face in place so she could not look away. Her fingernails dug into Rhea's skin. Rhea's eyes grew as wide as an observant tarsier. Her mouth dropped open, shocked. She did not try to resist Ava's hold or turn away from her glare. She was stuck there, looking into the eyes of a woman she had despised since she was a malnourished twelve-year-old, living in the Dust Bowl of northern Texas.

"She's been wanting to speak to you." Ava's face and all of its movements were now identical to Rhea's mother, from her crooked nose and bushy eyebrows to her port-wine birthmark that covered her ear and traveled down her neck to the top of her collarbone. Everything was as she remembered, except for the voice. It was still Ava's voice that she heard when she spoke.

Tears dripped down Rhea's thin face like collected dew on a car window. Rhea croaked.

"Aninan Translatio." The rings on Ava's back slowed down as Rhea's mother transferred from Ava to Rhea. Rhea's eyes shut tight, her body trembled, and then she collapsed motionless on the catwalk.

Ava fell back onto her butt. Her forehead beaded up with sweat. Next came all the aches and pains she had acquired since she took her first steps into the factory. Once again, Ava was exhausted beyond measure. The night had been long, but the sweet dawn was closing in. And for once, that thought was right. Within an hour, the sun would rise and thirty minutes after that, her mission would be over. Tired or not, Ava would have to climb those last set of stairs and make it to the kitchen, her final destination.

Ava felt a hint of elation as she climbed to her feet, grunting on her way up. Her arms quivered as they pushed against the metal grating. The prospect of finally ridding herself of the dead horse she had been dragging along for all these years was not enough for an extra boost of energy. All the souls were gone. They played their part in the end by making a huge sacrifice for another to possibly obtain their salvation.

Ava looked up to the broken Skylight that covered a quarter of the factory's southside ceiling. The black night sky was split open by a few colossal rays of intense light that seemed to pierce the Earth's crust. There were six of them in total, shining down from different angles, that made their way through the Earth's plane to the Abyss's Rings.

One ray for each level they forced their way through to each of the six souls that would soon be saved from the depths of the Abyss. They were like luminous pillars, standing tall and stark against the still starry sky. The sight was marvelous and miraculous all at the same time. A true sight to behold.

Only people like Ava, like the followers of the Abyss or her opposites, the Light Bearers, would ever see those pillars of light. The rest of the mid-westerners who had been close enough to see those colossal light rays, or even hear the chaotic commotion that had occurred throughout the night, would continue to sleep soundly, never knowing what had transpired in the dead miner's town of North Forks.

The events of that night were hidden from their senses. There were rules, and even though Ava had turned her back on the Abyss and their agents' extreme drive to exact revenge to claim their prize, those rules would be followed. A war was coming. It was inevitable, but it did not have to start up now. Not over a few stolen souls, taken by one insignificant Traveler.

Ava looked down at Rhea. Her eyes shifted back and forth under closed lids. Her arms and legs jerked periodically like a sleeping puppy dreaming of some great chase. What was she seeing? Ava would never know. Whatever kind of conjuring that Rhea's mother may have created in her daughter's mind, Ava was sure that it was not of the pleasant variety.

Guilt and a hint of sorrow passed over Ava's mind like a soft breeze. The years that they had spent with each other, no matter how she looked at it with perfect hindsight, had meant something. They changed Ava. They molded her. Initially for the worst, but if her actions throughout this tumultuous night made any difference in her stained past, the lessons granted to her from being under Rhea's wing had also produced some bits of positivity. Rhea had been a part of her since the beginning and now, almost by her hand, Ava had cut their ties for good.

And with that, those emotions blew passed like brooding clouds over a deserted beach. Ava was on her own now. All of the souls that pledged themselves to her cause had fulfilled their obligations. And as promised, they will be saved from the tortures of Hell and the fury of its inhabitants.

Now it was her brother's turn. Ava crossed the catwalk, steadied by the railings, to the stairwell's door. Slamming the metal door behind her, Ava leaned against it to get a much-needed breather.

Erik McGowan

-18-
DUMBWAITER

The hardest part is behind me.

Ava's body shifted like a well-crafted metronome. Her eyelids were heavy, weighed down with the sandman's expensive baggage. Ava fought to keep her eyes open as she climbed the stairs. Ava grabbed the metal rails as if she were holding on for dear life. She practically pulled herself up each flight as she climbed the stairs one step at a time. Her heavy lumbering steps echoed through the cemented stairwell.

Her last surprise for the Greys and straggling demons would wipe them out in one quick motion. Her whole night led to this moment. *This should be enough.* She hoped more than she had ever in her entire life. The plan, without its hiccups, had worked out so far. Six souls were saved from the depths of the Abyss, and one more to go.

Ava could not remember Levi's voice anymore, but she knew that memory was still in there somewhere. He would not leave her, and she could not let him down. He was the first sacrifice. The one that sent her down this path. It was a twisted ride that lasted twelve long years and slowly approached eternity. That was a fact that the Abyss and its Initiates did not tell her when she climbed aboard. No disclaimers were disclosed by the sinister operators. They just smiled and waved Ava on with the rest of the naive youth that followed along. The young have always been the easiest to convince.

Ava remembered watching Rhea Kane recruit new souls. It did not seem wrong at the time. She was helping them. In Ava's eyes, those new Greys were lost in this dull world, and they would be their guides to fun and excitement. Ava did not sit them down in the seat or strap them in, but she still carried the weight of helping to set them on that path. If she had never found out about her baby brother, Ava would still be in one of the front seats, riding along, swinging her feet while she ate sweets, oblivious of the upcoming dangers.

The trap had been set and she was nearly ensnared. But now, Ava had a trap for them. It took years of planning and studying to get this far. With this last seal, Ava the Fraud would purge herself and every single demon, Grey, Initiate, and Traveler that set foot in this dead town. Once this main seal was released, it would cause a chain reaction with all the other seals she placed within or near the structures. It would be the last sacrifice to complete her nocturnal journey.

Ava opened the metal door, partially rejuvenated from her slow ascent. The room was narrow. Cabinets and heavy-duty metal shelves lined the walls before the hall opened to the main section of the kitchen. Several feet in front of her, on the opposite wall, was a metal dumbwaiter with its tiny door open. She limped her way through the short hall towards the other side of the kitchen. Ava zig-zagged to make use of the shelves, a stainless-steel counter, and whatever else was close enough to keep herself stable.

The door slammed shut behind her. Ava paid it no mind. The door was heavy and the construction on this floor was never finished. She did not notice but the door's closer probably had not been installed yet since the doorknob was also missing.

Pain.

The piercing pain was instantly followed by a burning sensation. It was an ache unlike any she had felt before. Ava stopped in her tracks. Adrenaline pumped through her body, clearing away her fatigue within a split second. Ava's senses were heightened with the influx of hormones. Her pupils dilated and her vision became sharp and crisp. The air felt cool as her body instinctively inhaled a full capacity of air, fueling itself for whatever may come. The small hairs on her arms stood on end like the feelers of an insect.

Ava turned to look for the cause. She felt the same pain again but this time in the back of her leg, somewhere between her hamstring and glute. Her knee buckled. Ava collapsed to her hands and knees, and then to her stomach. The new pain shot through the lower half of her body, cutting through the adrenaline that was meant to silence it. Her knees were like firecrackers from the unyielding collision with the floor.

Ava did not dare to turn around this time and possibly receive another injury in a more vital area. Her eyes stayed locked on her destination. Ava pulled herself across the floor. The blood that leaked from her wounds left a smeared trail on the tiled floor like the mucus behind a traveling slug. Ava inched her way with one pull at a time. *Why do I keep finding myself in this position?* Her heart raced.

A voice, above her, low in tone, spoke with joy and exuberance. "I got you."

The declaration froze her in place. Ava tried to assess the situation, but the pain did not want to take a back seat. "I got you." The words reverberated in her head. "I got you." Ava knew that voice. *Kyle Burrows? Why is he here?*

Kyle Burrows was one of the more popular students at Red Glen High. Kyle was not quite at the top of the hill, but he was nowhere close to the bottom of the pile. With his above-average popularity came plenty of admiration. Many people, including the principals, teachers, other school staff, and his teenage peers all agreed that he would be successful in whatever endeavor he chose to pursue after his schooling. And if to prove all of them right, Kyle Burrows aimed for the moon and managed to collide with the stars.

After his stellar high school career, Kyle left Montana to pursue a degree in Sports Medicine. He had always felt like a big fish in a very small pond and if he was ever going to 'make it' and get a statue or a street named after himself, Kyle would have to create his fortune somewhere else. He did not care where he went as long as he was nearby or in the heart of a big city.

Red Glen had always been a small town, but he still had some stiff competition. The little town raised several high-standing athletes including the basketball twins, Denny and Darrell Crump who played small forward and power forward respectively, and a track and field star, Bryce Covington, who excelled at the discus throw and the 400m hurdles. Bryce and Red Glen as a whole had high hopes of him qualifying for the 1976 Summer Olympics, but that dream was cut short by a freak accident involving an old tree, a tire swing, North Forks' River, and a bed of polished rocks.

Red Glen also had a locally celebrated thespian, Charlotte Minks, who went on to be nominated for best supporting actor in a period piece set in the Victorian age. She was forty-five years older than Kyle, but her name was still the talk of the town by the time he reached middle school.

One year into college, his academic career was ruined by the glints and glamour of the big city. He did not do too well with his coursework but his natural skills of reading the room and effortlessly taking over said room saved him from returning home a failure. After a few more years of making connections, Kyle Burrows returned to his hometown with an unused bachelor's degree in kinesiology and a plan to make himself and possibly a few others from Red Glen extremely rich.

Kyle Burrows was the brains behind the tourism boom and the revitalization of the North Forks proper project; all of the buildings that used to line its main street and the Eastern Snowberry Co.'s cast iron factory that sat close to the North Forks' River. With his silver tongue and connections, Kyle was able to convince more than half the township and the local government to invest in his new project. He brought in construction crews, architects, city planners, a few historians, and an environmental engineer to help bring together his vision. Both towns, Red Glen and the vacant North Forks, broke ground at once.

Less than a year later, the tourism boom began. People flocked to Red Glen for the newly created tours by the hundreds at first and then by the thousands. Some of those tourists were converted into new residents and stayed for the new jobs that were created. Red Glen's small population grew with over two hundred new citizens in a five-year time frame. Things were looking up for the town. The residents of Red Glen could not have been prouder of their native son. Kyle Burrows received an honorary key to the city, was named Red Glen's 'First Son', and the new park that was constructed near the Livingston Court House was named Kyle Burrows Square.

If Only For One Night

A few weeks after First's Fall parade, an annual parade that starts in the heart of Bearing, which is a few miles to the east over the Route 12 bridge, and ends its march at Red Glen's town center, Avalee Wilson came back into town.

Kyle stooped down beside her. "Do you remember my face? I've never forgotten yours. I could never forget." The man brushed some of her hair from her face. "With all that pain," he squeezed her face, pressing her fat cheeks into her clinched teeth, "must be hard to keep up the fraud. Let me see that scar," he said. "Does it still look like the good ol' Grand Canyon?" Kyle smiled as if it was the first time he had ever told that joke.

"Grand Canyon, Lady Scarface. Your scar looks like a zipper made by someone with the tremors. Look at that period pad on her face." Kyle ridiculed Ava every single day she came to school after the incident. Kyle and his pack of friends spread rumors around Red Glen High with little to no regard for the consequences.

The attack that left Ava scarred physically and mentally for life happened on a school trip. Her class traveled to the largest college in the state, Montana State University in Billings. The trip was part of a junior year tour that was supposed to be a month and a half long. The tour was designed to expose the upcoming graduates to the biggest colleges in their state and some of the more notable ones across the country. Their next stop would have been the University of Minneapolis in Minnesota. That trip would have been collectively their first time on an airplane and most of the students' first time crossing the state's lines. But after the assault, the rest of the trips were canceled.

The sympathy that should have come Ava's way after such a traumatic experience never showed up. Taunts, blame, and name-calling arrived in its place, and the one and only golden child of Red Glen's lower eastside, Kyle Burrows, led the invasion party. When Ava finally got tired of the name-calling and petty mental abuse, she withdrew from her peers, and when she got tired of the gawking eyes and whispers, Ava withdrew from the town itself.

"There it is," Kyle said.

Holding the spell had become too hard to sustain. Ava's fraud spell slipped away, exposing her damaged face to the world. Grey hairs crowded around her widow's peak and weaved their way through each chunky loc on her head like wild vines.

Ava swatted Kyle's hand away. A golden 'R' twinkled as it shook on his black braided bracelet.

"That's fine. That's fine. You can have that. I did stab you in the back." He stood back up and looked around the room. "I've been watching you all night crater face. I was in the tavern, right by the door. All the way in the back. I couldn't believe it when I saw you. Rhea didn't tell me who we were going after."

Rhea? Rhea brought you here?

"I would've been too anxious if she did," he continued, "I might have done something reckless. But when she mentioned where we were going, how could I say no." Kyle pulled out a toothpick from his jacket pocket and went to work on his incisors. "I saw you while you were outside, creeping around the buildings. I didn't stick around to find out if they caught you. I figured when Kizzy," he looked around as if she was somewhere in the room with them, "Kismet, found you again, she would finish the job. I hadn't been back to the Forks for sooooo long. I wanted to see how my old pet project was doing. Right place, right time as they say."

"You set up a lot of seals throughout the building but up here, there is only one. So, I waited, right over there." Kyle pointed over to the corner close to the stairwell door with his saliva-soaked toothpick. "You know, some people like to talk to themselves—aloud—when they think nobody is around. I thought you might…"

The loss of blood started to severely affect Ava now. Ava's mind drifted and her attention waned. She could hear him talking but her mind was translating only fragments. Nothing made sense. Every time Ava blinked, her mind wandered through the harsh memories of her past. They played on the back of her eyelids like a cinema projector.

Ava's eyes closed.

***

"You can either be an Initiate or be an Agent of Chaos, which will it be?" Betta asked.

"What's the difference?" Ava asked.

"Initiates find new Greys to join the ranks and climb down the Abyss. Rhea Kane chose that path. Being an Agent of Chaos has its own set of difficulties. Namely, the person you influence must be someone close. It must be personal. No strangers. You must know them, and they must know you. And then, you destroy their life. No killing and no maiming. If they die, it will be by their own actions, not by yours," Betta said. "Think on it. You still have time."

***

Ava's dark brown eyes reopened, stopping halfway through their transition.

Kyle was still in his monologue, "...and to get past Betta, I was surprised about that. She..."

Ava's eyes drifted closed again.

***

"It's time to choose," Betta said.

Ava walked over. Betta was sitting in a high-back wicker chair. It was the kind of chair you might see in a Blaxploitation movie or on the cover of a 70's funk album. Betta looked up from her dinner as Ava approached. "Sit. A child should never look down on their mother."

Ava did not put up a fight. She sat down on the naked floor. Betta smiled with approval. Melodic music hissed and popped as the record played on the turntable in the corner of the room. Blue Oud incense burned in two containers that hung from the ceiling on either side of

Betta. Betta leaned back into the chair and placed her hands on the armrests.

"Agent of Chaos or Initiate?" Betta waited for a moment. She picked up a piece of steak fat and tossed it into her mouth. She swirled the fat around her mouth like a small piece of peppermint candy and sucked at its flavors. "You have considered it. That much I can tell." She examined Ava's face. Ava's feelings and thoughts were as hidden as the position of the ace of spades in a brand-new sealed deck of cards. "This is no time to practice deception. Speak."

"Agent of Chaos," Ava said, as confident as a rooster in a pen full of hens.

She pulled out the spent piece of fat, its flavors now all gone, and flicked it back on her plate. Betta smiled. Her eyes twinkled with the candlelight. "Whose life will you corrupt? Which friend or associate are you willing to sacrifice?"

"Red Glen," Ava said. She squinted. The smoke was beginning to irritate her eyes.

Betta's brow tightened.

Ava continued. "All of them."

Betta gave a Duchenne smile, baring white teeth and pink gums. "Yes. That will work. That. Will. Work." Her laugh was hardy. Betta rocked in her chair. Its round base creaked. "Success through one or through many—it's all the same. The rings of the Abyss are open for everyone." Betta smiled again. She picked up another piece of fat from her plate and stuck it in between her gums and cheek like a pinch of tobacco chew.

Ava's first mark for corruption was Kyle Burrows. He was one of the individuals that tormented her the most after the park incident. In hindsight, when all things are 20/20, and if they are ever remembered correctly, he probably did not torment her the most. Memories tend to change and warp as time passes. The small memories of the past that play in a loop can sometimes overshadow moments of more importance. It could have been anyone else in the surrounding towns or anyone of her peers at Red Glen High who was high enough on the social ladder that was the real one causing all of her torment, but Kyle Burrows became a victim of his fame and notoriety. His nasty words and his stupid face had etched themselves into her memories until he became the figurehead of it all.

The corruption she was tasked to commit as an Agent of Chaos was not just to ruin a day in her target's life by inconveniencing them. The task was to cause the person so much grief that they could be turned into an unwitting chaos afflicter or an easy mark for an Initiate to turn. Being able to take revenge and test all of her skills including her newly learned charms sat well with Ava. She was excited about the assignment, but she did not want to push him or any who lived in Red Glen toward becoming a Grey. In her eyes, that would have been too kind of a gesture. She wanted to break Kyle Burrows and everyone around him. Ava wanted the whole town to crumble like North Forks did decades before.

So, when she ultimately caused the demise of Kyle Burrows, Ava made sure that all of his misgivings trickled down to the rest of Red Glen's citizens as well.

Within a few months, Ava did just that. Her actions and influence corrupted the whole town. She crushed the once popular tourist pit stop into what it was today; a struggling, 'could have been' town. Every semblance of prosperity was sapped away, leaving a third of the town practically barren. Two-thirds of Red Glen's folks were left penniless, mentally and emotionally exhausted, buried early in shallow graves, or broken through and through. Even the two surrounding towns, Bearing and Klink, who economically isolated themselves from North Forks after its first collapse, were still hit hard by Ava's heavy-handed blow to the region.

Ava's success came from the multitude of souls that were lost to the depths of the Abyss. Upon her return to her Den Mother after her chaos was sowed, Ava was promptly promoted to the rank of Traveler. With the eight-pointed star branded to her wrist, not two hours cooled, Ava opened her first fiery gate to the Abyss and climbed through.

***

"And then Rhea found me, sleeping in the vacant hotel on Clark Street. A bottle tucked under one arm and a needle in the other."

Hearing Rhea's name snapped Ava out of her stupor. *Rhea.* Ava thought back to when she saw Kyle's bracelet. The image was already becoming fuzzy at the edges, but the picture was clear in the area she needed to see. The 'R' medallion, for Rhea Kane, dangled from his bracelet.

The seal. Ava's inner voice was fatigued. She began to pull herself across the floor again. The pain was getting worse by the second and the dragging did not help a single bit.

"You're not going to last long like that," Kyle said.

Ava's smeared blood collected into tiny puddles. She was losing too much blood.

"Where are you going? Over there?" He pointed towards the far wall.

Ava did not respond. She kept moving, as fast as she could. Her body was as heavy as her eyelids. Breathing had become one of the hardest things she had ever done in her life, but she kept going. *Don't give up. Don't give up. Just a little bit more.*

"You were going to use that seal over there? And then what? You were going to be trapped too." Kyle laughed. He flicked the waterlogged toothpick at her body. "What were you going to do? Jump out of the window?" Kyle walked between two steel counters to the closest window and looked down to the ground below. He laughed some more, scratching at the back of his head. "You wouldn't survive that. That's got to be a sixty-foot drop. And I might add, there's nothing but concrete outside." He pointed. His index finger flexed from the pressure on the glass. "You would shatter your legs and your feet… probably destroy your pelvis, crack a few of your ribs from the compression, maybe destroy a couple of bones in your back and um, split your pants." He laughed at the idea, amusing himself. "Hm…" He looked around some more. His eyes slowly tracked around the room.

Kyle saw the two traffic doors that led to the unfinished dining space. The large windows that covered the south wall were covered in plastic to shield them from dust and paint during the construction process. "Oh." He elongated the word and then followed it with a short whistle. "I get it now." He winked at Ava. "The baby elevator…"

"Dumbwaiter," Ava said through the pain, not quite loud enough for him to understand.

The dumbwaiter sat snug in the brick wall between the two doors. It looked like a miniature steel elevator. The kind of elevator a rich aristocrat would have to transport their favorite miniature dog between floors of their house so it could avoid the struggle of climbing the stairs with their short legs.

"If I'm dumb, what does that make you?" Spittle rained down from his mouth, spraying some of her exposed skin like an aerosol. Kyle kicked Ava a few times in her unprotected ribs.

Ava curled up from the pain. All of the nerves in her body felt like they were on fire. It was like an arc of electricity jumping back and forth on every nerve in her body.

"I know what's going on." He tapped at his temple. "I've seen that seal before." He pointed at the glyphs on the wall. His face was turning red, and his eyes bulged.

A massive heptagon seal was etched into the drywall like one of Ava's many tattoos. The seal was lined with different types of glyphs and archaic letters. Its design could hardly be seen from the lack of light in the half-completed kitchen and because of the Fraud spell that encased it. But like with most things, the well-trained eye of a Traveler or Initiate can always detect the obscure.

The moon's time of dominating the night sky was finally coming to a close and so was Ava's window of opportunity.

"You were going to use that and escape in that thing. There's probably a delay or protection seal on it. Am I right?"

Kyle looked down and smiled with the cockiness of a self-professed know-it-all. He spotted Ava's fingers wiggling in her blood like a doodling child. His smile vanished in an instant. Kyle stomped on her right-hand several times with tremendous force. He stopped his barrage once he heard a couple of crunches from the metacarpals in her hand snapping.

Ava screamed, internally and externally. Her hand, mangled from the assault, trembled from the pain.

"That's a hard seal to make. Takes a lot of time. You must have planned all of this out. What's the trigger? Huh?"

Ava did not speak. She slowly rocked on the floor like a small rowboat stuck in choppy waters. She tried her best to keep the pain to herself. Ava did not want to give him any satisfaction, but she could not hold it back. She was in a lot of pain. *At least I'm not crying.*

"Doesn't matter," he said, "blood usually works." Kyle kneeled and wiped up some of the blood that was on the ground next to her. "I suppose... you wouldn't be in the mood to tell me how much time I have left. Am I right?"

Only muffled moans came from her body. Her legs felt cold. Her lower half tingled with pins and needles.

Kyle walked over to the heptagon and rubbed Ava's drying blood through the center of the seal with a quick swipe and then with a flourish wrote his initials in bold letters like a murderous John Hancock. The large seal cracked. A sizable fissure ripped its way through the smear of blood. The symbols at its edges grew in brightness like a warming light bulb. The new light lit up the rest of the room like a neon sign, allowing Kyle and Ava to see everything clearer. He raced over to the dumbwaiter as the glyphs at the edges of the heptagon wiggled like a tray full of gelatin during a massive earthquake. The glyphs and archaic letters rotated around the seal, slowly building up speed.

The Eastern Snowberry Co. factory, which had stood in some form or another for over one hundred years, had begun to fall to pieces. Tiles from the kitchen's white foam drop ceiling fell, bouncing off the stoves and grills. Fissures raced across the floor and up the walls. A few of the windows shattered. Their glass salted the kitchen floor. Cool air from the mountains rushed in through the newly opened holes. The metal door that Kyle hid behind for his ambush, jerked back and forth on its hinges like the chomping of some metal-jawed monster. Through the doorway's open maw, the groan from the twisting catwalk echoed off the brick stairwell.

The destruction did not stop with the factory. Explosions from outside could be heard in the distance. The plastic that covered the dining hall's windows shook from the concussive winds. Flames engulfed the tavern and the surrounding buildings. The North Forks' arch that marked the entrance to the town collapsed as parts of its frame snapped. Car alarms cried out into the night. A tremendous boom could be heard through the floor from the giant ladle being dislodged from the ceiling and crashing to the ground below.

"Next time I'm in Hell, let me know how your spell turned out," Kyle said. He stuffed himself into the compact dumbwaiter. It was a tight fit, but his forced position would be comfortable enough for his short ride. He only had a couple of flights to go and then he would be off to the races.

His knees were pressed tight to the sides of his cheeks. Kyle twisted his neck just far enough to see Ava's bloody body lying still on the floor. He reached out, slapped the round, down arrow button, and then forced his arm back between his legs. The dumbwaiter shook a tiny bit as its motor kicked in. "Bye-bye now." Kyle waved with just his fingers before the dumbwaiter's door closed and his metal carriage descended to the safety of the first floor.

Five minutes had passed since Kyle Burrows took his trip down in the metal dumbwaiter. The factory had fallen silent once again. The light that beamed from the seal on the wall had died out. The cracks that zig-zagged across the walls disappeared like the fallen tiles that had split into pieces on the tops of the appliances and stoves. The orange glow that brightened North Forks in the night from the fires that raged through the town had also faded away. And the shiny stainless-steel dumbwaiter that Kyle Burrows had climbed into to escape Ava's fate had reverted to the dingy, rusted, death trap that it always was.

When it was originally installed, several decades ago, the dumbwaiter never worked properly. It routinely got stuck halfway between floors during its short transit through its shaft. Shotty construction and planning led to frequent water leaks into the shaft, which over time, damaged the pulley system. The construction crew that Kyle hired for the renovations, Ready-Set Construction, decided that repairs for the dumbwaiter and its shaft would be too expensive for the budget that the town had, and it ultimately did not serve any purpose. So, they decided to hide the whole system in the wall, which went against Kyle's directive of keeping everything as close to the original feel as possible. The lower levels were already sealed shut, but the kitchen floor was never finished. So, the dumbwaiter's entry point, to Kyle's detriment, was still exposed.

The natural rope that operated the lift had been rotting in solitude for decades. With Kyles's extra weight, the pulley system's rope snapped after only traveling down a single floor. Kyle's claustrophobic ride slowed and then ground to a halt in the middle of the second floor's warped walls. The tight box that Kyle forced himself into, the dumbwaiter, was now his metal coffin. Kyle squirmed as much as he could, but he was stuck. He yelled and screamed as he pushed at his enclosure to free himself to no avail. Two feet of reinforced brick and deformed steel stood firm to the measly force he could muster. The confined space also left him unable to move enough to open a gate or to create any meaningful glyphs.

Pride.

It tends to sneak up on you. It catches you by surprise. Pride seeps through the tiniest cracks, destroying your foundation, until it finally destroys you.

Ava laughed to herself after he took off down the dumbwaiter. She had always been good at fraud spells. The laugh, though short-lived, brought the most relief she had gotten throughout the night. Even after Gluttony's seal was released and all of her pain and fatigue had left her body, it could not compare to those few seconds of laughter. Once they were over though, the pain came crashing back in, maybe worse than before. Her broken hand trembled as she tried her best to avoid putting any pressure on it.

Ava lay there, halfway on her side, resigning herself to death. It came for her on its pale white horse, screaming like a banshee. Ava could feel the horsemen and his sickly steed creeping up on her. She could hear the thumping of its hooves as he approached. Ava was so tired. She was tired of running and tired of fighting. There was nothing else she could do but wait.

All of the voices were gone. *I saved six.* She was happy about that. *Some are always better than none.* But her ultimate goal was to save her little brother, and now he will be stuck in the bowels of Hell for all of eternity because she could not finish the job. She was so close. Ava was not going to be able to pull herself across the room to the seal she crafted specifically for this night. She was not going to get her chance to release it for the salvation of her brother. And Avalee 'Bug' Wilson, the fraud, the destructive Traveler, the stubborn daughter, and the protective sister, was not going to live long enough to see the sunrise.

She cried. Tears of grief, tears of pain, and tears of defeat streamed down her face.

The bright sun rose over the snowcapped mountains in the distance. Its amber glow washed over the factory, over both towns, North Forks and Red Glen, and all of their surroundings. The rays pierced through the factory's windows, causing the remaining demons that lurked in the shadows of the machines or who scoured the forest, to retreat to their realm. Ava grew paler as time progressed with the rise of the golden sun. As it rose, so did the rays. They slid across her tattered body like a spotlight, warming her.

In that warmth, she forgot about the pain from the two metal skewers that were still lodged inside her, about the chaotic night that proceeded this inviting morning, and all about the miss deeds and transgressions she had done for decades while she traveled for the Abyss. Her stressed mind and her disfigured body had finally relaxed. Ava's heart rate slowed, and her eyes drifted closed for the last time, ending the final chapter of her tumultuous life.

Within that instant, between life and death, that split second that some say can span your entire existence, Ava finally saw the truth. She finally understood why her little brother Levi was taken. Through all of those years, she had put all of the weight of his abduction on her shoulders. She had always felt as though it was her fault; indirectly, but her fault, nonetheless. If she had not become so rebellious or climbed the Abyss, his soul would have still been there, in the land of the living. And she would have been there with him; scars and all.

But that was not the truth. The truth was heavier than that—much heavier.

***

"I will always watch over you. I promise," Ava said. With a quick jab, Ava poked her wrist with a sharp pocket knife.

The abandoned Eastern Snowberry Co. factory's rigid figure watched with its cracked windows from less than a mile away in the distance. The sun had been riding low in the sky for twenty minutes. Their hike to this secluded location was a two-and-a-half-hour trip, mainly because Levi was occasionally sidetracked from watching the wild animals that roamed about in the clearings or glided from tree to tree.

The knife was given to her by her mother in secret as a welcome home gift from the hospital. "Here." Ava's mother slipped it into her pants pocket. "Sometimes we have to protect ourselves, or others." She tried to smile. All of the worry a mother holds for her child's future and safety was barely hidden on her face.

Blood bloomed from the punctured skin, almost as thick as paint. Levi's face flinched as he watched his sister with fear and curiosity. He instinctively knew what pain looked like or what could cause it, but he had never seen blood oozing out of someone before, not even in the movies. Their parents kept those types of movies away from him. Ava mixed the blood with some charcoal she made with a ten-cent lighter she found beside a trashcan outside of the local bank, and a few dry sticks and leaves she tasked Levi to collect during their trip along the river.

The next prick was on her brother. "This is going to hurt," Ava said. She used a sewing needle and her blood ash mixture to mark Levi behind his ear where their parents would never notice. He squirmed from the pain, but he did not run from it. Ava was proud of him and his bravery.

Right then and there, next to the North Forks' River and about a fifteen-minute walk from the factory's decaying, graffiti-written walls, Ava completed her first binding spell, linking their two fates together like an expertly crafted dovetail. A piece of her soul was now and forever connected to him and a piece of his was now with her.

"Nothing is free. We all make sacrifices. All of us." Rhea was right. From the very beginning, Ava's soul had been on the offering block in exchange for the new life she led with the Abyss. Those payments were extracted from her year after year as she climbed deeper into the Abyss. And one of those payments was paid with a piece of herself that existed in her brother. By including Levi in her new life out of selfishness, Ava had condemned her little brother to an everlasting eternity of torture and torment.

-19-
EPILOGUE

Ava's eyes opened to the black. No stars were twinkling in the darkness and there was no moon lazily drifting along. Her head hurt. The pain throbbed at the nape of her neck and spread over the back of her skull like a brush fire. She reached behind and dislodged a rock that existed between her neck and the ground. Sweet relief came just as quickly as she removed that jagged stone. Ava tossed it to the side. The clacking sound of stone against stone echoed around her as if she were in a vast cave or canyon.

Ava sat up, massaging her neck as she looked around at her surroundings. Everything was flat, in every direction, as far as she could see. There were no trees, no buildings, no mountains, or hills. No grass or bushes or even animals. There was nothing for her to see to give her any sign or landmark to help her pinpoint her location. She looked again at what should have been the sky. Not a single light source to be seen but the environment around her was as bright as an overcast day.

A large fog appeared in front of her, creeping low to the ground. Ava peered into it. Where did it come from? How did it come to be? There was nothing there except for herself and the rocks she sat awkwardly on. Ava picked up another one of the rocks and examined it. Everywhere she looked in the distance it was pitch black but somehow, she had no issue seeing the rock. She made out its color and shape with no great effort at all. Ava could even make out its texture.

How?

Just inside of her periphery, Ava thought she saw something moving in the distance. She stared into the gray cloud, looking for any hint of movement. Ava shot up to her feet after feeling something slide up against her legs. The perceived movement and whatever rubbed against her legs jolted her heart. Ava grew hot in a split second. Her throat went dry. Rocks clicked and crunched under her bare feet as she shifted her weight, preparing to run.

Ava reluctantly looked down to where she felt the unknown touch her. It was water. Dark uninviting water lapped at the edge of the fog. The water was almost as black as whatever hung above her head or watched her from a distance in almost every direction.

In the distance, far out into the fog, Ava saw movement again. The shadow appeared like an apparition, slowly growing in size as she watched. Ava squinted in hopes of helping her see better. The squinting did nothing to aid her in uncovering what was hidden by the shadows, but she continued to squint anyway. As the shadowy area grew, the fog that surrounded it expanded at the same rate. Where the fog was once maybe fifteen feet away, though she really could not tell because of the circumstances, it was now drifting past her knees.

A boatman with a face wrapped with tight, jerky-like skin, stood on a high platform at the stern, sculling the vessel with a large oar. He rocked as he maneuvered the oar back and forth. The rhythm was as gentle as a swaying baby in the arms of a grandparent. The boatman stared blankly at what must have been the coast where Ava stood. His eyes were almost completely white from what looked to be cataracts. A leather pouch dangled from his belt. Its shape bulged as if it was filled with an innumerous number of objects.

The thickness of the fog continued to drift in closer with the boatman and his wooden ship. The lumbering cloud almost engulfed Ava with the chill of an autumn morning. Ava stepped back several times, removing herself from its cold climate. Her hands nervously rubbed themselves in a cleaning motion. She did not know what to do. Flight was the first option on her list, but where would she go? The world around her was a vast land of nothingness. There was nowhere to go to and nothing to hide behind or sneak inside.

Ava could feel her heart beating faster and faster. She continued her slow retreat, not taking her eyes off the approaching ship. The half-dead-looking captain and the ominous fog continued their slow advance. Her withdrawal continued until she left the stony shore. Ava's feet could no longer feel--anything. She looked down towards the ground that should have been there. Her eyes could see her naked feet with their thin toes but nothing else. She felt like she was standing in the midst of space, billions of miles away from any of the stars that usually clutter the sky. Ava scrunched up her toes to try to feel any sensation to give her mind some kind of comfort, but those ten digits found absolutely nothing. Ava was standing in nothing itself.

The sound of the boat beaching on the rocks brought Ava's attention back to her earlier concerns. Its hull creaked and moaned as it beached itself on the smooth rocks. She looked up to see the fog that once encompassed the area in front of her had receded as quickly as it appeared earlier. The boatman did not say anything. His skinny arms rested on the end of the long oar. His wispy hair made a crown on his oddly shaped head.

Water gently splashed against the shoreline. A young-looking passenger in a pair of dark pants and a baggy long-sleeved white V-neck shirt made its way to the bow. They hopped off the side of the ship like a rebellious teenager leaping over a waist-high turnstile and splashed down into the murky water with no regard for what might be below the surface. Before Ava could get a clear look at their face, the passenger turned away and pushed at the bow of the ship to dislodge it from the rocky shore. She could see the flexing of their muscles as they pushed at the heavy load.

If Only For One Night

The boatman watched on, never leaving the stern. He smiled down at her from his platform. His dust broom eyebrows rounded as the corners of his eyes creased. After a couple of strong shoves, the boat broke free of the polished stones. Its wooden hull rocked as the black waters embraced its full weight. Ava watched as the boat drifted back into the dense fog until it was concealed within its opaque form.

The passenger gave a quick wave to the ship, before wiping their hands on the front of their pants. "You did it," the passenger said before turning around to face her.

Ava could not quite recognize the face, but something seemed familiar. Over the years, throughout her climb, Ava has seen hundreds of thousands of people, and she still remembered all of them. All of their faces had been seared into her memory. Was it the curly hair that covered his head or his big floppy ears that caused them to stick out to the side? Maybe it was his dark skin and thin eyebrows that reminded Ava of her father. Or was he more like a figure in a dream? The appearance might not match up but something about them lets you know exactly who they truly are.

"Levi..." The name forced its way out of her mouth.

Levi had a manly face, full of whiskers and wisdom beyond the years she had last seen him. Several moles cluttered his face, just below his dark brown eyes. He smiled with the brightest smile she had seen in decades. Even though he was much older, Ava remembered that crooked smile like it was yesterday. She cried out to him, arms stretched, ready for an embrace.

They ran at each other, eyes full of tears, blubbering like children. Her head slammed into his chest. His arms wrapped around her shoulders like a cloak. They squeezed. The embrace was long and tight. Ava reached up and grabbed Levi's face, kissing his cheeks and forehead. He did not pull away or put up a fight.

Ava struggled to get the right words out through her tears. She had been waiting, hoping for this moment for years, and it had finally arrived. For months on end, Ava planned out what she would say to him when she saw him. She would lay everything out for him at that very moment. Everything she had been holding onto since she left her parent's house, through to the moment she saw him trapped in the ice, but her planned speech never left her lips.

She was too overwhelmed by their reunion. Ava apologized profusely. "I'm sorry. I'm so sorry. They came for a part of my soul and found it in you." Ava kissed him a few more times. "I'm sorry." It was all too much for her to stay calm.

"I forgive you," Levi said.

Ava believed him. His loving words were enough to snap her back from her hysteria. She wiped her eyes as she gathered her thoughts. "Where am I?" It was the first question she had since she woke up with that stone pinned behind her neck.

"Purgatory," Levi said with a sniff. He wiped his face to clear his cloudy skies.

If Only For One Night

"Purgatory…" It was her first time within the borders of Purgatory. The space was off-limits to everyone who climbed the Abyss, but Ava knew of its stories. Purgatory was the eternal waiting room where nothing but yourself would be there to keep you company and the doctor would never be ready to see you. Ava looked around at the vast empty space. "Alone." Her heart knocked around in her chest. She did not want to be alone, not for an eternity. She would take the torture of the lower rings over something like that. "No—"

"You will not be alone forever. This is a realm of your making. It's what you have created for yourself. A self-inflicted punishment. You can escape from it, in time."

How long? She dared not ask. Ava wanted to know the answer, but she did not want to hear it. She had been alone long enough while she was with the living. Repeating that same cycle in death was a terrifying thought.

"I can't tell you how long," he continued. "That is up to you. When do you think it should be over? How long before you have paid off your debt?"

"Now." The words jumped out of her mouth. "Right now."

Levi looked around at the emptiness that persisted. "You don't believe that."

Ava wanted to believe he was wrong. She wanted this whole situation to be a mistake, or some fever dream brought on from an infection caused by the blade that sliced open her face, but Levi was right. She did not truly believe her words.

"I can't stay." Levi put his hand on her shoulder. It was heavy. As heavy as any weight she had borne throughout her long life. "I'm sorry," he said.

She knew that he could not stay but she did not want him to leave. "Don't say that. I'm the one who is sorry. I'm the reason for all of this. I destroyed our lives, and our parent's lives because I couldn't…," The tears welled up in her eyes once again.

"I forgive you Avalee," he reminded her. "And I'm sure they do too."

Forgiveness, was it something that she could accept? Could she ever really deserve it? Ava's mind battled with itself on that notion. She had caused some much pain and grief to not only her immediate family but also to thousands of others throughout the world.

"We are linked," Levi said. "It's a bond that has never been broken." He rubbed the back of his ear with his thumb. Ava looked down at the two black dots on the inside of her wrist. Each one looked like a tiny mole or birthmark. "It's still here." He reached over and grabbed Ava's wrist. "I can still hear you. I know how you felt, Avalee. And at times, I know you could feel me too."

Ava's eyes overflowed as she nodded in agreement.

"I also know that you have been through a lot already. But you are going to make it through." Levi wiped some of the tears from her face.

His palms engulfed her chubby cheeks as he held her face. "You saved six souls and mine by sacrificing your own. You are worthy. Remember that, Ok?"

A column of light shot down like a lightning bolt, splitting the dark mass that was above them, and engulfing her brother in its brightness. She stared up at him. Her eyes strained to keep focus through the light's intensity.

Levi smiled. "Forgive yourself, Avalee. Forgive yourself. Turn this void into the world that you would want to live in. Escape your prison."

Within a split second, the column of light vanished, and Levi was gone. Ava was alone once again. She looked around for the boat, but it had been long gone like the shoreline of polished rocks, the black water, and the thick fog. Nothingness stretched out around her like the endless sands on the Ring of Frauds.

Ava sat down, finally resigning herself to her new reality. She had saved him, just like she wanted, but she lost everything else along the way. It was probably the best outcome she could get for all that she had done, but it did not make her circumstances any easier to accept. He was gone and she was here, stuck.

Ava did not try to walk through Purgatory's vast emptiness in hopes of finding some secret trapdoor that her brother might not have known about. She knew it would be a mistake much like those desert wanderers scouring the landscape in search of shade or some water to quench their thirst. Acceptance has always been the first step to true change.

Ava's mind went back to the man in the suit, traveling across the endless dunes. *Andre, right?* She wondered how he was doing. *Why didn't he accept the offer?* His choice still puzzled her. *He was so determined to make it on his own. Did the Others ever catch up with him?* Ava felt sad for him. He could have been saved by now if he had just accepted her help. He would have been freed from his hardships like the other six souls. Instead, he decided to roam for the rest of eternity, tortured by the extreme heat and the baking sun, in search of salvation. Ava shook her head at the thought.

"Struggle until you can't anymore," Ava heard him say. "...until you can't anymore."

Keep struggling. She smiled with her whole face for the first time in years. I'm going to be all right. "I'm going to be all right," Ava repeated out loud. The words soothed her aching heart much like the kind words of forgiveness from her little brother. Ava looked up.

A point of light, no larger than the head of a pearl sewing pin, twinkled in the blackness.

***

THANK YOU FOR READING THIS NOVEL. IF YOU ENJOYED "IF ONLY FOR ONE NIGHT", PLEASE LEAVE A REVIEW WITH THE PLACE OF PURCHASE OR ANY OF YOUR FAVORITE BOOK REVIEW SITES.

PLEASE CHECK OUT MY FIRST NOVEL, "MAGNANIMOUS ABSOLUTION". BE ON THE LOOK OUT FOR MY NEXT UPCOMING PROJECTS COMING SOON.

Made in the USA
Middletown, DE
03 April 2024